George B. Thayer

Ancestors of Adelbert P. Thayer, Florine Thayer McCray and Geo. Burton Thayer

children of John W. Thayer and Adaline Burton - also, reminiscences of a Christmas

Eve at Windermere and some early events in the life of the writer

George B. Thayer

Ancestors of Adelbert P. Thayer, Florine Thayer McCray and Geo. Burton Thayer
children of John W. Thayer and Adaline Burton - also, reminiscences of a Christmas Eve at Windermere and some early events in the life of the writer

ISBN/EAN: 9783337381660

Printed in Europe, USA, Canada, Australia, Japan

Cover: Foto ©Andreas Hilbeck / pixelio.de

More available books at **www.hansebooks.com**

ANCESTORS

OF

ADELBERT P. THAYER,

FLORINE THAYER McCRAY,

AND GEO. BURTON THAYER,

CHILDREN OF

JOHN W. THAYER

AND

ADALINE BURTON.

COMPILED BY

GEO. BURTON THAYER.

ALSO,

REMINISCENCES OF A CHRISTMAS EVE AT WINDERMERE
AND SOME EARLY EVENTS IN THE LIFE
OF THE WRITER.

EDITION LIMITED TO FIFTY COPIES.

No 6-

In Honor

of

MY FATHER AND MY MOTHER

AND IN

Memory

of

OUR HOME AT WINDERMERE,

AND OF OUR OLD DOG,

"BRUISER,"

THIS WORK WAS DONE.

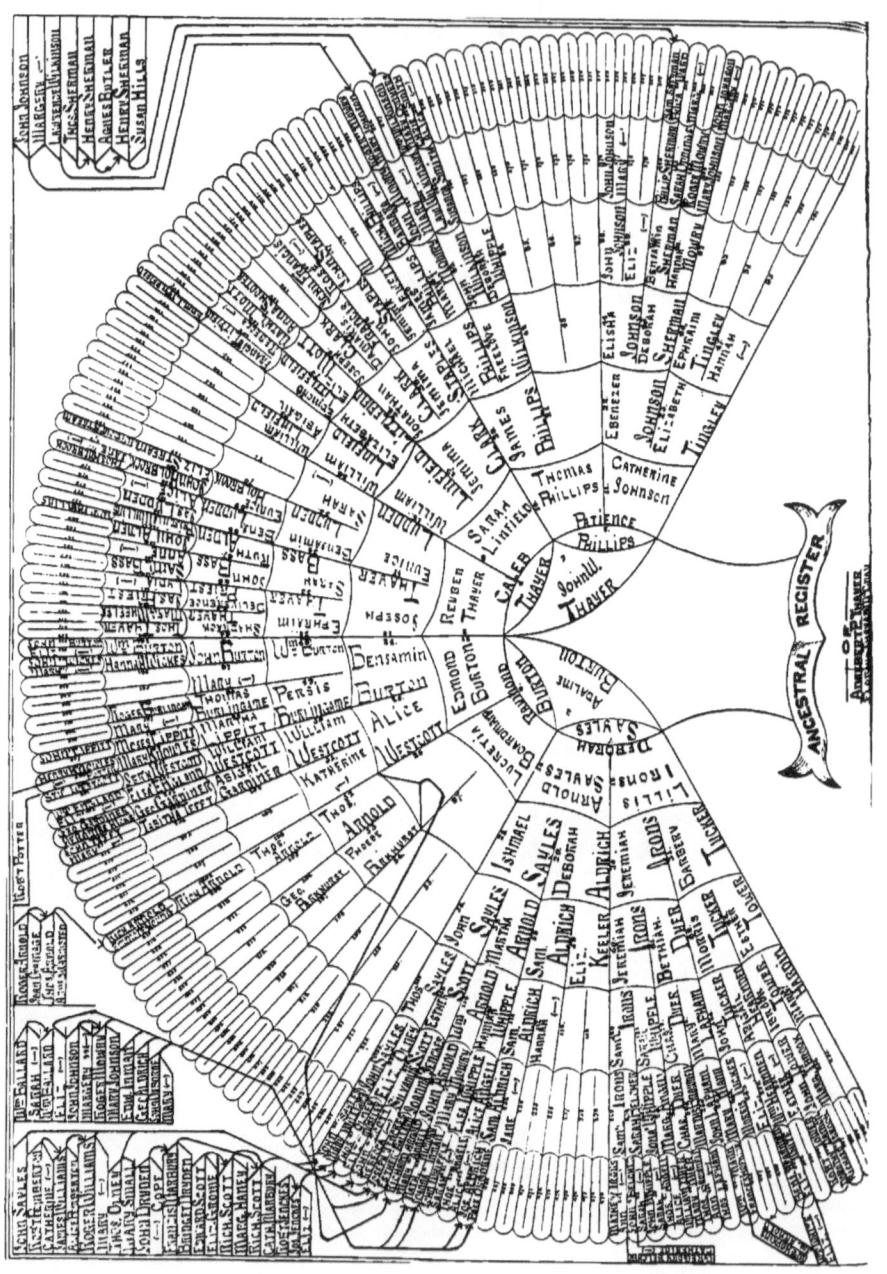

ANCESTRAL REGISTER
OF

PREFACE.

HIS WORK was begun during a brief summer vacation, for the purpose, at first entirely personal, of tracing out one or two ancestral lines, but success in one line served only to whet the appetite for wider knowledge, and the work soon became so fascinating the writer could not rest content until, with the result of researches made, from time to time, during a period of two years, he had "rushed into print." The writer, however, wishes to acknowledge, just here, the debt of gratitude which he owes to other and earlier workers in genealogy. Their work is done and many of them have now taken their places in the ancestral lines, but the fruit of their labor has fallen to us.

In looking over the records, the writer has not turned aside to avoid any unpleasant discovery, and it is worthy of note that, among the three hundred or more sketches, no flagrant crime will be found mentioned, with the solitary exception, in the old Puritan times, of one arrest for licentiousness.

In the "Summary of Events," under the head of "Ancestors in New England before 1650," the fact appears that all but nine of the fifty-nine families mentioned in the book had arrived and settled in this country previous to that early date.

In the list of "Graves of Ancestors Located," those only have been included that have been visited and identified by the writer.

The accompanying register or chart, while necessarily considerably reduced in size from the original, may assist the reader in the study of the different relationships.

The wealth of genealogical information accessible at the Conn. Historical Society was a surprise to the writer, and he gratefully acknowledges the courtesies extended at that institution.

In following down the different converging lines of descent, the writer has been perplexed to select, from so many, a family coat of arms, seeing that now they all vest in him, but, unable to choose from the abundance, the book appears with none.

Hartford, Conn., December, 1894.

SUMMARY OF EVENTS.

The leading events referred to in the accompanying
ancestral sketches are herewith briefly summarized:

(6)

SUMMARY OF EVENTS.

(7)

SUMMARY OF EVENTS.

ANCESTORS IN NEW ENGLAND BEFORE 1650.

Alden, Aldrich, Angell, Arnold, Ballard, Bass, Belcher, Brownell, Burton, Dyer, England, Francis, Gardiner, Hearnden, Hicks, Holbrook, Hopkins, Ibrook, Inman, Irons, Jenckes, Johnson. Knowles, Lapham, Lippitt, Littlefield Ludden, Mann, Mott, Mowry, Mullins. Olney, Osborne, Parkhurst, Potter, Priest, Sayles, Scott. Sherman, Smith, Staples, Stream, Thayer, Tower, Westcott, Whipple, White, Wickes, Wilkinson, Williams

LENGTH OF ANCESTRAL LINES.

Extent to which the different families have been traced back without a break in the line.

The family of Arnold, 28 generations.
The family of Jenckes, 21 generations.
The families of Dryden, Pemberton, Scott and Sherman, 12 generations.
The families of Ballard, Johnson, Parkhurst and Williams, 11 generations.
The families of Aldrich, Belcher, Hopkins, Inman, Mowry, Olney, Osborne, Potter, Sayles, White and Wilkinson. 10 generations.
The families of Angell, Brownell, Burton, Dyer, England, Gardiner, Hearnden, Holbrook, Ibrook, Irons, Knowles, Lapham, Lippitt. Littlefield. Mann, Mullins, Smith, Tefft, Tower, Westcott, Whipple and Wickes, 9 generations.
The families of Alden, Bass, Burlingame. Francis, Johnson, Ludden, Mott, Phillips, Priest, Staples, Thayer and Tucker, 8 generations.
The families of Clark and Linfield, 7 generations.
The family of Tingley, 6 generations.
The family of Boardman, 4 generations.

(8)

Alden.

JOHN ALDEN, said to have been the first to leap upon Plymouth rock, and known to have been the last male survivor of the passengers of the Mayflower, was not of the Leyden Church party, but "was hired for a cooper at Southampton (England), where the ship vituled and being a hopful yong man was much desired but left of his own liking to go or stay when he came here but he stayed and maryed here." He was the youngest of the party, half of whom (fifty) perished at Plymouth within the year, and he also attained the greatest age of any. Soon after landing he married Priscilla Mullins, the only surviving member of a family of five, her father, William Mullins, mother, brother and servant, all dying from the suffering and hardships encountered by the Pilgrims the first winter. John Alden afterwards became a prominent man in the early settlement of the Massachusetts colony, always performing the public duties imposed upon him with credit to himself and satisfaction to the colony. He died at Duxbury, September 12, 1687, at the age of 90, "in good old age, an old man and full of years, and was gathered to his people, and his sons buried him." The "Courtship of Miles Standish," the early records of the Massachusetts colony, and other literature regarding him, all easily accessible, make further mention of John Alden here unnecessary.

RUTH ALDEN, daughter of John and Priscilla (Mullins) Alden, was born at Duxbury, Mass., and married December 3, 1657, John Bass, son of Samuel and Ann (——) Bass, of Rox-

(9)

ALDEN.

bury. They settled at Braintree, where she died December 8, 1674.

DESCENT.	Ruth Alden	married	John Bass;
whose daughter,	Sarah Bass,	"	Ephraim Thayer;
" son,	Joseph Thayer,	"	Eunice Ludden;
" "	Reuben "	"	Sarah Linfield;
" "	Caleb "	"	Patience Phillips;
" "	John W. "	"	Adaline Burton.

Aldrich.

GEORGE ALDRICH, the progenitor of one of the oldest Rhode Island families, and said to be a scion of the English nobility, came from Derbyshire, England, in 1631, and first settled and joined the church at Dorchester, Mass. An entry in his diary reads as follows: "God brought me to America from Derbyshire, in England, November 6, 1631." In 1640 he had removed to Boston, and from 1644 to 1663, he was a resident of Braintree. He then removed to Mendon, being one of the first settlers He remained there during the remainder of his life, excepting a year or two spent at Swansea in 1669–70, and a brief stay at Braintree during the King Philip war. His wife was Catherine (——). He died in 1682.

JOSEPH ALDRICH, son of George and Catherine (——) Aldrich, was born at Dorchester, Mass., June 4, 1635, and married Patience Osborne, of Weymouth, daughter of John and Mary (——) Osborne, February 26, 1662. Captain Torey, of Weymouth, officiated. In 1687, after a brief stay at Braintree, they moved to Providence, R. I., where he died in 1701. A sword is found among the items in an inventory of his estate.

SAMUEL ALDRICH, son of Joseph and Patience (Osborne) Aldrich, was born at Braintree, Mass., about 1664, and married Jane (——), about 1681. They moved to Providence. R. I., with his father, in 1687. He was a tanner by trade, and in 1706 had eleven shillings, three pence's worth of leather taken from him "for not training, he being a Quaker." In 1733 he removed to Smithfield, where he died April 2, 1747. Among his assets were bills of public credit amounting to £184. His wife, Jane, died soon after.

ALDRICH.

SAMUEL ALDRICH, son of Samuel and Jane (——) Aldrich, was born at Braintree, Mass., in 1681, and came first to Providence, R. I., and later to Smithfield, with his father. He married Hannah (——), about 1710, at Providence, and died at Smithfield, March 28, 1761. Nothing further is known of his wife.

SAMUEL ALDRICH, son of Samuel and Hannah (——) Aldrich, and known, to distinguish him from his father and grandfather, as "Swearing Sam" Aldrich, was born at Providence, R. I, May 4, 1722, and went to Smithfield with his father in 1733, where he married Elizabeth Keeler, about 1745. She was an Englishwoman, but little else can be learned about her. During the Revolutionary war he was 5th ensign in and later captain of the 2nd company of Smithfield militia. He was also a member of the town council. This branch of the Aldrich family, while otherwise above reproach, was noted for many exhibitions of violent temper and a frequent use of profane language, so much so that they were called "Hornbeam Aldriches." This name, hornbeam, is said to have first been applied to them as the result of an expression used by the subject of this sketch on a certain occasion, to wit: He was standing in his front door one day watching a thunder storm, when the lightning struck a hornbeam tree in his front yard, damaging it, however, scarcely any. Seeing how effectively the tough species of timber had resisted the power of the lightning, Sam is said to have exultingly exclaimed:

"God, you got your match that time, didn't you?"

Thus did the family come to be known as the "Hornbeam Aldriches," and it is claimed the scarcity of the tree in recent years is accounted for upon the supposition that the timber has all been used up in making Aldriches, since a numerous race.

"Swearing Sam" is credited with another anecdote illustrating his irrepressible nature, which, aside from this habit,

ALDRICH.

was not, however, bad. One day the recently ordained pastor of the church, a stranger to Sam, but not to his profane propensity, started out to call on him and met him not far from home.

"My good friend," said the clergyman, "can you inform me where a man lives who is known in the neighborhood, I am sorry to learn, as 'Swearing Sam Aldrich?'"

The object of the clergyman's search, without a moment's hesitation, replied: "Jesus, God, I'm the man." Captain Samuel Aldrich died in November, 1802, and in 1894 the writer found his grave, among others, on the brow of a hill an eighth of a mile east of the Metcalf Comstock homestead, two miles southwest of Woonsocket, on the road from Union Village to Tarkiln. The farm is south of the road and slopes to the north.

DEBORAH ALDRICH, daughter of "Swearing Sam" and Elizabeth (Keeler) Aldrich, was born at Smithfield, R. I., July 12, 1750, and married Ishmael Sayles, son of Colonel John and Martha (Arnold) Sayles, of Smithfield, October 7, 1773. They settled on a farm on Buck Hill, in the town of Burrillville, where she died May 19, 1810. Her grave, with that of her husband and one child, could be found in 1894 on the old farm situated near the main road running from Pascoag to East Thompson, Conn., two and one-half miles west of Pascoag. The graves were a short distance off in the lots to the north of a lane leading west from a cross road running south, about a quarter of a mile from the main road above mentioned. The farm was in 1894 known as the "Staples farm." The headstone gave her age as 63 years. She was a woman of slight frame, with a thin, sharp face, but a great worker. When her husband went to the defense of the colony, during the Revolutionary war, she, with two small children, and her son, Arnold, then a mere boy, were left to do the farming. With the help of a hired boy of fourteen, they did the haying, the hired boy

(18)

doing the mowing and the mother and her boy tedding and raking after. The day of the battle of Rhode Island, August 29, 1778, in which her husband was engaged, they were thus at work, the sound of the booming cannons being heard by them out in the hay-field, even at that distance.

DESCENT.	Deborah Aldrich	married	Ishmael Sayles;
whose son,	Arnold Sayles,	"	Lillis Irons;
" daughter,	Deborah "	"	Raymond Burton;
" "	Adaline Burton,	"	John W. Thayer.

Angell.

THOMAS ANGELL, the early companion of Roger Williams and the first of the family name to settle in Rhode Island, was the son of Henry Angell, of Liverpool, England, and came to this country in the ship "Lyon," from Bristol, arriving at Boston in December, 1630. He first settled at Salem, but in 1636, with four others, came with Roger Williams to Providence, R. I., arriving there earlier than July. The previous winter had been spent at Seekonk. He was then a young lad living in the family of Roger Williams, whose only companion he was in that first memorable trip up the Providence river in a canoe. The next year, although still a minor, he signed the famous civil compact with twelve others.

In 1656-7 a Massachusetts officer came to Pawtucket, arrested a man and attempted to return with him to Boston. The Providence authorities, hearing of it, sent Constable Thomas Angell, with others, one of whom was John Sayles, to rescue the prisoner. They found the Massachusetts officer at a house where he was to remain over night. The officer thus relates the occurrence: "About 10 o'clock comes in Thomas Angell, the constable of Providence, and a sergeant with four men more for to apprehend my body and Richard Chasmor, who was then our prisoner." The matter was argued at some length, with the result that the prisoner was finally released.

At the close of the King Philip war Thomas Angell was on the committee that recommended the conditions under which the Indian captives were disposed of by the towns. They were required to serve those plucky inhabitants of Providence and Warwick who, upon being invited to seek shelter on the island of Rhode Island, "stayed and went not away." Besides being constable, he served as town clerk, juryman and commis-

(15)

sioner. In 1694 he died, first making careful provisions in his will for his widow's welfare. Among other things, he stipulated that his son, James, should give her another cow, and the "keep of same" when the one given her by his son, John, had "become unfit for milk by age."

ALICE (——), his wife, was probably born in England and came to this country early in its settlement. They were married at Providence about 1645. Her economy appears from the fact that when her husband died there were found "1,000 pins" among the household goods, and, at her death, a year later, the same 1,000 pins were a part of the inventory of her estate. Apparently not one had been lost. She died at Providence in 1695.

MARY ANGELL, daughter of Thomas and Alice (——) Angell, was born at Providence, R. I., about 1645, and married Richard Arnold, son of Thomas and Phœbe (Parkhurst) Arnold, of Providence, about 1668. She died in 1695 at Providence.

DESCENT.		Mary Angell married Richard Arnold;
whose son,	John Arnold,	" Mary Mowry;
" "	William "	" Hannah Whipple;
" daughter,	Martha "	" John Sayles;
" son,	Ishmael Sayles,	" Deborah Aldrich;
" "	Arnold "	" Lillis Irons;
" daughter,	Deborah "	" Raymond Burton;
" "	Adaline Burton,	" John W. Thayer.

ALICE ANGELL, daughter of Thomas and Alice (——) Angell, was born at Providence, R. I., in 1649, and married Eleazer Whipple, son of John and Sarah (——) Whipple, of Providence, January 26, 1669. She died at Smithfield, R. I.,

(16)

ANGELL.

August 13, 1743, at the age of 94 years, having outlived her husband 24 years.

DESCENT.		Alice Angell	married	Eleazer Whipple;
whose daughter,		Hannah Whipple,	"	William Arnold;
"	"	Martha Arnold,	"	John Sayles;
"	son,	Ishmael Sayles,	"	Deborah Aldrich;
"	"	Arnold	"	"	Lillis Irons;
"	daughter,	Deborah	"	"	Raymond Burton;
"	"	Adaline Burton,	"	John W. Thayer.

MARGARET ANGELL, daughter of Thomas and Alice (——) Angell, was born at Providence, R. I., about 1665, and married Jonathan Whipple, son of John and Sarah (——) Whipple, of Providence, about 1687. She died at Providence, about 1700.

DESCENT.		Margaret Angell	married	Jonathan Whipple;
whose daughter,		Sarah Whipple,	"	Samuel Irons;
whose son,		Jeremiah Irons,	"	Bethiah Dyer;
"	"	"	"	"	Barbery Tucker;
"	daughter,	Lillis	"	"	Arnold Sayles;
"	"	Deborah Sayles,	"	Raymond Burton;
"	"	Adaline Burton,	"	John W. Thayer.

Arnold.

ROGER ARNOLD, according to the pedigree recorded in the College of Arms, in England, descended from Ynir, King of Gwentland, who flourished in the 12th century and who was paternally descended from Ynir, second son of Cadwalader, last King of the Britons. King Cadwalader built Abergavenny, in Monmouthshire, and the castle was afterwards rebuilt by Hamlet, son of the Duke of Balladon of France. Portions of the wall still remain. Cadwalader, by one account, died at Rome in 688. Somerby's genealogical researches in England shows that Ynir, King of Gwentland, by his wife Nesta, daughter of Jestin ap Gurgan, King of Glamorgan, had a son Meiric. The descent, somewhat abbreviated, is as follows: Meiric's son was Ynir Vichan, whose son was Carador ap Ynir Vichan, whose son was Dyfnwall ap Carador, whose son was Systyl ap Dyfnwall, whose son was Arthur ap Syssylth, whose son was Meiric ap Arthur, whose son was Gwillim ap Meiric, whose son was Arnholt ap Gwillim, whose son was Arnholt ap Arnholt Vychan, whose son was Roger Arnold of Llanthony in Monmouthshire, the first of the family name to adopt a surname.

Roger Arnold married Joan, daughter of Sir Thomas Gamage, Knight, Lord of Coytey. Their son was Thomas, who succeeded to Llanthony and other estates. He married Agnes, daughter of Sir Richard Warmstead, Knight. Their second son was Richard, who removed into Somersetshire and resided in the parish of Street. He married Emmote, daughter and heir of Pearce Young, of Damerham, in Wiltshire, by whom he had three sons. One of them, Richard, removed to Dorsetshire and became seated at Bagbere, parish of Middleton, otherwise called Milton Abbas. His manor house at Bagbere was standing till 1870, when it was demolished. He was twice

(18)

ARNOLD.

married and died in 1595. Thomas, his second son, lived for a time at Melcombe Horsey, from which place he removed to Cheselbourne and seated himself on an estate previously belonging to his father. His first wife was Alice, daughter of John Gulley, parish of Tolpuddle. By his second wife he had Thomas, born April 18, 1599. Thus has the family in England been traced back seventeen generations.

THOMAS ARNOLD, son of Thomas Arnold of Cheselbourne, England, was one of the early settlers of Watertown, Mass., where he was repeatedly fined for offenses against the established religion. He was born at Cheselbourne, Dorset County, England, in 1599, and came to America in the ship "Plain Joan" in May, 1635, first landing in Virginia, and returning to Watertown. His first wife died either before or soon after reaching this country, and, about 1640, for his second wife, he married Phœbe Parkhurst, daughter of George and (——) Parkhurst, of Watertown. In 1651 he was fined twenty shillings for an offense against the law concerning baptism; again, in 1654, £5 for neglecting public worship twenty days, and again, in 1655, £10 for neglecting the same for forty days. In 1661 he sold his farm and removed to Providence, R. I., where he was chosen a member of the town council and was five times appointed deputy. He died in September, 1674, leaving a large estate in lands. His nephew, Benedict Arnold, great-grandfather of the traitor, refers in his own will to "my stone built wind mill" in town of Newport, which, from its location, is believed to be the famous stone mill in that place.

RICHARD ARNOLD, son of Thomas and Phœbe (Parkhurst) Arnold, and one of the public men of his day, was born at Watertown, Mass., March 22, 1642. He came to Providence, R. I., with his father, at the age of nineteen, and, soon after, married Mary Angell, daughter of Thomas and Alice (——)

(19)

ARNOLD.

Angell, of Providence. He was twice a member of the town council, nine times an assistant and thirteen times a deputy, the last two years, 1707–8, acting as speaker of the house of deputies. He was on the committee appointed to draw up an address of congratulation from Rhode Island to James II. upon his succession to the crown. In December, 1686, he was appointed by Sir Edmund Andros a member of his council, and attended the first meeting of the council held at Boston. In 1695 he was chosen, with two others, to run the northern line of the colony. He died April 22, 1710, leaving in his will a provision that his son, Thomas, should have the service of the negro, Tobey, till the slave was twenty-five years of age, when Tobey should be given his freedom and also "two suits of apparel, a good narrow axe, broad hoe and sickle."

JOHN ARNOLD, son of Richard and Mary (Angell) Arnold, and one of the wealthy men of Rhode Island, was born at Providence, November 1, 1670, and about 1693 married Mary Mowry, daughter of Nathaniel and Joanna (Inman) Mowry, of Providence. He was a miller by trade and about 1712 built his corn and fulling mill on the island near Woonsocket Falls. Being a Quaker, he had twelve shillings' worth of pewter taken from him in 1706 "for not training." In 1719, he was appointed to build the Quaker meeting-house, which was to be twenty feet square and "the height thereof left to him." He also sold an acre of land, about the same time, situated, the record says, "near the place formerly called the dugway, whereon is a burying place of people called Quakers." In 1731, he had removed to Smithfield, and was a member of the town council. He died at Smithfield, October 27, 1756, leaving an estate valued at nearly £10,000. Among the items inventoried were "three pairs of nippers to draw teeth," and a Bible, with a book of Apocrypha, valued at £12. His first wife died January 27, 1742, and October 31, the same year, he married Hannah Hayward.

ARNOLD.

WILLIAM ARNOLD, son of John and Mary (Mowry) Arnold, was born at Providence, R. I., December 9, 1695. He married Hannah Whipple, daughter of Eleazer and Alice (Angell) Whipple, of Providence, December 27, 1717. He was twice appointed deputy, in 1721, and again in 1738. He removed to Smithfield about 1732. He was allowed £75 towards the expense of building a bridge across the Pawtucket River at Woonsocket Falls, and a few years later was made a director in a lottery authorized to raise £2,000 to rebuild the bridge. In 1742, he was appointed one of a committee to try a gang of counterfeiters. He died at Smithfield, August 2, 1766.

MARTHA ARNOLD, daughter of William and Hannah (Whipple) Arnold, was born at Providence, R. I., December 28, 1721, and married Colonel John Sayles, son of Thomas and Esther (Scott) Sayles, of Smithfield, December 19, 1742. The date of her death can not be given.

DESCENT.	Martha Arnold	married	John Sayles;
whose son,	Ishmael Sayles,	"	Deborah Aldrich;
" "	Arnold "	"	Lillis Irons;
" daughter,	Deborah, "	"	Raymond Burton;
" "	Adaline Burton,	"	John W. Thayer.

JOANNA ARNOLD, daughter of Thomas and Alice (Gulley) Arnold, of Cheselbourne, Dorset County, England, was born November 30, 1577, and about 1600 married William Hopkins, of the same town. She probably died in England.

DESCENT.	Joanna Arnold	married	William Hopkins;
whose daughter,	Frances Hopkins,	"	William Mann;
" "	Mary Mann,	"	John Lapham;
" "	" Lapham,	"	Charles Dyer;
" "	Bethiah Dyer,	"	Jeremiah Irons;
" son,	Jeremiah Irons,	"	Barbery Tucker;
" daughter,	Lillis Irons,	"	Arnold Sayles;
" "	Deborah Sayles,	"	Raymond Burton;
" "	Adaline Burton,	"	John W. Thayer.

(21)

Ballard.

WILLIAM BALLARD, a farmer from London, England, sailed in 1630 in the "Mary and John," Captain Sayres, and settled at Lynn, Mass., with his wife, Sarah, and several children. When the celebrated military organization, the "Ancient and Honorable Artillery Company," was first organized in 1638 he was one of the original members. He was appointed magistrate in 1638. He died about 1643. A day or two before his death it is recorded that he intended to make his will the next day, but died before he could put it to writing. He would have his wife, Sarah, have half, and his children the other half of his estate.

WILLIAM BALLARD, son of William and Sarah (——) Ballard, was born in England in 1603 and sailed from London in 1635 in the ship "James," with his wife, Elizabeth, and one child, Esther, then two years of age. He settled first at Lynn, Mass., and later at Andover, where he was a considerable land owner. He died at Andover, July 10, 1689. One of his sons, Joseph, has the notoriety of being the cause of the first charge of witchcraft against citizens of Andover during that strange and horrible craze. His wife had been sick for many weeks and medicine brought no relief. Her husband finally decided to try the so-called spiritual methods for ascertaining the cause of her ailment. Accordingly, he sent to Salem and induced two of the party of young girls, who were engaged in that strange work there, to come over to Andover. They were received with great solemnity, and were immediately conducted to the meeting-house, where a season of prayer followed. They were then abjured to tell the truth, and, upon being questioned, named certain persons in Andover and other places as tormentors of the sick woman. The constable, another son of

BALLARD.

William Ballard, forthwith obtained warrants for the arrest of the accused, and hurried them off to Salem jail. Others were accused, and in a short time forty prisoners were placed in irons and huddled together in the limited space within the jail. The story of the horrible affair need not be retold. In all, eight Andover citizens were condemned, three were hanged and one died in prison, not to mention the victims from other towns.

ESTHER BALLARD, daughter of William and Elizabeth (———) Ballard, was born in England in 1633, and at the age of two years was brought to this country by her father in the ship "James," from London. She married Joseph Jenckes, son of Joseph Jenckes, of Lynn, Mass., about 1652. In 1652, soon after her marriage, she was "presented" at court, charged with "wearing silver lace." In 1669 they went to Warwick, R. I. Two years later they removed to Providence, where, in 1717 or later, she died.

DESCENT.		Esther Ballard	married	Joseph Jenckes;
whose daughter,		Joanna Jenckes,	"	Silvanus Scott;
"	"	Esther Scott,	"	Thomas Sayles;
"	son,	John Sayles,	"	Martha Arnold;
"	"	Ishmael Sayles,	"	Deborah Aldrich;
"	"	Arnold "	"	Lillis Irons;
"	daughter,	Deborah "	"	Raymond Burton;
"	"	Adaline Burton,	"	John W. Thayer.

Bass.

SAMUEL BASS, one of the prominent churchmen of the early Massachusetts colony, was born in England, in 1600, and came to this country, with his wife, Anne, and one or two children, about 1630. He first settled at Roxbury, near Hog Bridge, and there became one of the earliest members of the first church, which was organized in 1632. In 1640 he removed to Braintree, where he held the position of deacon in the church for half a century. He was once offered the position of ruling elder, but declined. He was a man of strong and vigorous mind, and a leading man in the town, representing it in the General Court for twelve years. He was appointed by the town "to end all small cases" at court involving a sum under twenty shillings. The custom of using home-made beer as a substitute for tea and coffee was common in those days, and the malt for making the beer was usually procured from Deacon Bass. In 1659 an action was brought against two citizens of Braintree "for giving John Frizell so much liquor as made him drunk and occasioned his miserable freezing." The complainant in this case was the dealer in malt, Deacon Bass. He died December 30, 1694, the progenitor, before his death, of 162 children. His wife, Anne, died in 1693, age 93 years.

JOHN BASS, son of Samuel and Anne (———) Bass, was born at Roxbury, Mass., about 1632, and moved to Braintree with his father, in 1640, where he married Ruth Alden, daughter of John and Priscilla (Mullins) Alden, of Duxbury. The marriage ceremony was performed by "Mr. John Aulden," December 3, 1657. John Bass died at Braintree, September 12, 1716, age 84.

SARAH BASS, daughter of John and Ruth (Alden) Bass, was born at Braintree, Mass., March 29, 1672, and married

(24)

BASS.

Ephraim Thayer, son of Shadrach and Deliverance (Priest) Thayer, of the same town, January 7, 1692. She died at Braintree, August 19, 1751. In a twenty-four verse poem, written at the time of her death and found in full in several genealogies, it is said she and her husband "like two lambs they did agree and pulled together in one yoke. She was a fruitful vine, fourteen was of her body born, and lived to man's estate. From those did spring a numerous race, one hundred thirty-two, sixty and six each sex alike. And one thing more remarkable, she had fourteen children with her at the table of the Lord."

DESCENT.	Sarah Bass	married Ephraim Thayer;
whose son,	Joseph Thayer,	" Eunice Ludden;
" "	Reuben "	" Sarah Linfield;
" "	Caleb "	" Patience Phillips;
" "	John W. "	" Adaline Burton.

Belcher.

GREGORY BELCHER came from England to this country in 1634, and first settled at Boston, Mass. He soon after removed to Braintree, where, about 1640, he assisted in founding the first church. He afterwards owned the land where the first iron foundry was located in America in 1640. His wife, who probably came from England with him, was Catherine (——). He died at Braintree, November 25, 1674. She died in 1680, or soon after.

JOHN BELCHER, son of Gregory and Catherine (——) Belcher, was born at Braintree, Mass., about 1635, and married Sarah (——), about 1655. They settled at Braintree, where he died in 1694. The town, December 24, 1694, appropriated "£5 for John Belcher's widow's maintenance."

SARAH BELCHER, daughter of John and Sarah (——) Belcher, was born at Braintree, Mass., June 27, 1656, and married Samuel Irons, son of Matthew and Ann (——) Irons, of Braintree, November 13, 1677. She died, probably, at Braintree.

DESCENT.	Sarah Belcher	married	Samuel Irons;
whose son,	Samuel Irons,	"	Sarah Whipple;
" "	Jeremiah "	"	Bethiah Dyer;
" "	" "	"	Barbery Tucker;
" daughter,	Lillis "	"	Arnold Sayles;
" "	Deborah Sayles,	"	Raymond Burton;
" "	Adaline Burton,	"	John W. Thayer.

Boardman.

Lucretia Boardman was born in 1764, and about 1785–90 married Edmond Burton, son of Benjamin and Alice (Westcott) Burton, of Cranston, R. I. In personal appearance she was a handsome woman and in her manners very lady-like. She suffered for years from a cancerous tumor, but finally died of consumption, November 12, 1815. Her grave in 1894 was beside that of her husband in the Benjamin Burton family burying ground, situated about two miles and one-half west of Cranston, on the road to Hope, by the old furnace. The ground is about one-third of a mile from the main road, on the east side of a cross-road running north up a hill from the main road. Her name on the stone is "Lucrety."

DESCENT. Lucretia Boardman married Edmond Burton;
whose son, 　　Raymond Burton, 　　''　　Deborah Sayles;
　''　daughter, Adaline　　''　　　　''　　John W. Thayer.

(27)

Brownell.

THOMAS BROWNELL, one of the early Rhode Island settlers, was chosen water bailie in May, 1647, at Portsmouth. In 1664 he was elected deputy, and in 1655–61–62–63 commissioner. He died in 1665. His wife was Ann (——), and she survived him.

MARTHA BROWNELL, daughter of Thomas and Ann (——) Brownell, was born in May, 1643, probably at Portsmouth, R. I., and, for her second husband, married Charles Dyer, son of William and Mary Dyer, of Newport. She died at Portsmouth, February 15, 1744, nearly 101 years of age.

DESCENT.	Martha Brownell	married	Charles Dyer;
whose son,	Charles Dyer,	"	Mary Lapham;
" daughter,	Bethiah "	"	Jeremiah Irons;
" son,	Jeremiah Irons,	"	Barbery Tucker;
" daughter,	Lillis "	"	Arnold Sayles;
" "	Deborah Sayles,	"	Raymond Burton;
" "	Adaline Burton,	"	John W. Thayer.

Burlingame.

ROGER BURLINGAME came from Stonington, Conn., to Warwick, R. I., in 1660, having lived at Stonington at least since 1654. In 1671 he removed to Providence, and continued to live there, although elected a deputy in 1690 from the town of Warwick. This election was declared illegal, "after much debate in the assembly," and it was ordered that "he is not accepted." He died at Providence, September 1, 1718. His wife, Mary (———), died about the same time.

THOMAS BURLINGAME, son of Roger and Mary (———) Burlingame, was born at Warwick, R. I., February 6, 1667, and married Martha Lippitt, daughter of Moses and Mary (Knowles) Lippitt, of Warwick, about 1687. After living at Providence for a time he settled at Cranston, where he died July 9, 1758.

PERSIS BURLINGAME, daughter of Thomas and Martha (Lippitt) Burlingame, was born at Cranston, R. I., August 14, 1703, and married William Burton, of Cranston, son of John and Mary (———) Burton, February 8, 1722. She died at Cranston, June 22, 1772.

DESCENT.	Persis Burlingame	married	William Burton;
whose son,	Benjamin Burton,	"	Alice Westcott;
" "	Edmond	"	"	Lucretia Boardman;
" "	Raymond	"	"	Deborah Sayles;
" daughter,	Adaline	"	"	John W. Thayer.

Burton.

JOHN BURTON, "Gentleman," of London, England, is believed to be the father of the first settler in Rhode Island of that family name. John Burton was a man of considerable property, and died December 7, 1626, leaving his estate to his wife, Elizabeth Handcorne, and to his son, William. To his wife he gave the lease of certain tenements on the mill bank at Westminster, and the lease of certain cellars under the long armory on Milk street. To his son he gave his manor of Barons in Essex, and all lands, meadows and tenements situated in the parishes of Purleigh and Haseley in Essex. In default of his son's issue, one-half of his share was to go to the Company of Vintners, and one-half towards maintaining the preachers at Powles Crosse, London, and the poor of St. Brides als Bridget, London, equally. To his son he also gave his sword, inlaid musket, bandoleers and horseman's pistols, and all his Latin and French books, as well as the prayerbook his father left him. To a knot of cousins, fourteen in all, he gave £4 to pay for a supper for them, and to each he gave 10 shillings to buy them bandstring rings to wear in remembrance of him.

His wife, Elizabeth, was appointed administratrix during the minority of his son, William. Upon reaching his majority, May 22, 1640, William took upon himself the executorship of the estate.

WILLIAM BURTON, son of John and Elizabeth (Handcorne) Burton, of London, England, came to Providence, R. I., early in its settlement. About 1650 he married Hannah Wickes, daughter of John and Mary (——) Wickes, of Warwick. He lived on the north side of the Pawtucket river, and in 1662 was granted the privilege of buying land from the Indians. He died February 20, 1714. His second wife, upon her death

BURTON.

in 1722, granted their mulatto woman, Jane, a featherbed, several worsted combs, a spinning wheel, and her freedom.

JOHN BURTON, son of William and Hannah (Wickes) Burton, was born at Cranston, R. I., May 2, 1667. About 1690 he married Mary (——). In 1702 he is on record as having given three shillings towards building a Quaker meeting-house at Mashapaug. In 1716 he was chosen deputy. In 1749, July 15, he died, leaving an estate valued at £2,512. This included £735 in bonds and "a negro man and his apparel, £300." His wife married again and died at Cranston, December 29, 1768. In his will he gave his wife the use of the dwelling house at Chestnut Hill, and to his son, William, "the homestead farm where my honored father William, late of Providence, deceased, dwelt, at Mashanticut." This homestead was situated about two and a half miles west of Knightsville, on the direct road to Kent, upon a broad, high hill, called Applehouse Hill, commanding a magnificent view to the east of Providence and Narragansett Bay. At night, from this point, the boats passing down the bay and the lights of Fall River, twenty-five miles away, can easily be seen. The place in 1894, known as the Brown farm, was a fine one, on the south side of the road, the house being situated up at the end of a branch road. The family burying ground was located in the center of a large pasture to the east of this branch road, but the remaining uninscribed graves, a few years ago, were ploughed over, and no distinguishing marks now are left of the graves of John Burton or his father William.

WILLIAM BURTON, son of John and Mary (——) Burton, was born at Cranston, R. I., about 1700, and married Persis Burlingame, daughter of Thomas and Martha (Lippitt) Burlingame, of Cranston, February 8, 1722. In 1735 and in 1742 he was appointed deputy, and between 1743 and 1750 was five times chosen assistant. In 1754, when the town of Crans-

(81)

ton was set off from Providence, he was the first justice of the peace and town clerk of the new town, and besides being deputy again, afterwards served as town clerk for many years. He died at Cranston, January 3, 1773.

BENJAMIN BURTON, son of William and Persis (Burlingame) Burton, was born at Cranston, R. I., November 4, 1739, and, December 25, 1755, at the age of 16, married Alice Westcott, daughter of Captain William and Catherine (——) Westcott, of Cranston. He probably died at the old Burton homestead, in the town of Cranston, or on a portion of the farm a mile to the south of the old homestead, where he is believed to have lived.

EDMOND BURTON, son of Benjamin and Alice (Westcott) Burton, was born at Cranston, R. I., November 25, 1763, and married Lucretia Boardman about 1785–'90. He was a blacksmith by trade, and one of the wealthy men of the town. He was a great singer, of a lively disposition, and in his old age was said to be quite "clever." In August, 1799, the town council voted "to license Edmond Burton to sell strong liquor in any quantity in his house on September 11 and 28, in order to accommodate the infantry company in that district and the Cranston Blues—to pay $1 therefor—money paid."

After the death of his wife in 1815, he made frequent visits on foot to his friends and relatives, in the neighboring towns, always carrying a cane with a dog's head carved upon the handle. Once, in a fit of resentment, he threw himself on the town, but only for a short time. He died December 19, 1844, and lies buried in the Benjamin Burton family burying ground, situated about two and one-half miles southwest of Knightsville, by the old furnace on the road to Hope. The burying ground is about one-third of a mile from the main road on the east side of a cross road running north up a hill from the main road. The headstones which in 1894 plainly marked his and his wife's graves, were ordered by his son, Raymond, who, however, never went near them afterward. The stones were finally placed in position by Alice Burton, daughter of John Anthony Burton and niece of Edmond.

RAYMOND BURTON, son of Edmond and Lucretia (Boardman) Burton, was born at Cranston, R. I., February 22, 1795, and married Deborah Sayles, daughter of Arnold and Lillis (Irons) Sayles, of Chepachet, May 6, 1814. He was well educated, a fine penman, and of a scientific turn of mind. He also acquired a knowledge of law, and was frequently consulted by his neighbors. In business, however, he was not so successful. He settled in Chepachet, afterwards living for a time at Burrillville and Waterford. In constructing a dye-house at Burrillville, he fell, one day, and struck his head against the building, injuring his brain so seriously as to cause insanity years afterwards. In personal appearance he greatly resembles President Martin Van Buren. He died April 13, 1871, and lies buried on Acote's Hill, in Chepachet.

Adaline Burton, daughter of Raymond and Deborah (Sayles) Burton, and mother of the writer, was born at Chepachet, R. I., January 29, 1823. When the family removed to Waterford, Mass., she went to the Bank Village Academy, and later finished her education at the Smithville Seminary, at North Scituate, in 1841. In 1843, April 2, she married John W. Thayer, a wool sorter at Waterford, and son of Caleb and Patience (Phillips) Thayer, of Sterling, Conn. The Rev. Maxy Burlingame, of the Free Will Baptist Church, united them in marriage. After living successively at Rockville, Windermere, and again at Rockville, upon her husband's appointment as clerk at the Connecticut Hospital for the Insane at Middletown, she made her home with the writer at Vernon, in 1879, and removed with him to Hartford, in 1887. She was always known as a woman of rare integrity of character, systematic methods, and of intellectual tastes. Her love of reading was her greatest pleasure through life, and her lively interest in current affairs a distinguishing characteristic. She began the reading of the Chatauqua course after she was sixty years of age, and at the end of four years received her diploma. Whatever literary talent her children may have displayed was largely inherited from her. She had no relish for personalities or small gossip, and, even in the midst of her frequent illnesses, could always forget her ailments to discuss the latest scientific discovery or advanced religious thought, the newest book or any up-to-date fad or fancy. She was a self-constituted member of the Humane Society before such an organization was in existence, and many instances are on record where she interfered to protect and care for suffering animals. While demanding a high moral course in her family and friends, she was not censorious to unfortunate ones, but lent them a helping hand accompanied by much sound advice as to their future conduct. She was essentially a product of Puritan New England, though somewhat softened and liberalized by experience. In 1894 she was still living.

Clark.

JOSEPH CLARK married Damaris Francis, daughter of John and Rose (——) Francis, of Braintree, August 19, 1675. He lived, and probably died, at Braintree.

JONATHAN CLARK, son of Joseph and Damaris (Francis) Clark, was born at Braintree, Mass., March 14, 1689, and married Jemima Staples, daughter of John and Jemima (Jewett) Staples, of Braintree, October 5, 1711. In 1730, he petitioned the town for a new highway to his farm. In 1735, he served as constable, and in 1739 he was appointed to inspect the killing of deer. He died, probably, at Braintree.

JEMIMA CLARK, daughter of Jonathan and Jemima (Staples) Clark, was born at Braintree, Mass., January 7, 1721, and married, about 1742, William Linfield, son of William and Elizabeth (Littlefield) Linfield. She died, probably, at Braintree.

DESCENT.			
	Jemima Clark,	married	William Linfield;
whose daughter,	Sarah Linfield,	"	Reuben Thayer;
" son,	Caleb Thayer,	"	Patience Phillips;
" "	John W. Thayer,	"	Adaline Burton.

Dryden.

JOHN DRYDEN. The Drydens, of Canons Ashby, came to the county of Northampton, England, originally, from the neighborhood of the Scottish border. They were of decided Puritan principles, and Sir John Dryden, great-grandfather of the English poet, was noted as a staunch parliamentarian. His house lay obnoxious to the Royalist garrison of Towcester, on the one side, and Banbury on the other, and on at least one occasion a great fight took place within stone's throw of the house. The parliamentarians barricaded themselves in the church at Canons Ashby and defended it and its tower for several hours before the Royalists forced the place and carried them off prisoners. The house is still in possession of descendants of the family on the female line, and is delightfully situated, looking like a miniature college quadrangle set down by the side of a country lane, with a background of park in which deer wander, and a fringe of formal garden, full of the trimmest of yew trees. Sir John Dryden, about the middle of the 16th century, married Elizabeth, daughter and heiress of Sir John Cope, Kt. of Canons Ashby, and by her had at least two children, Sir Erasmus Dryden, Bart., grandfather of the poet, and Bridget.

BRIDGET DRYDEN, mother of Ann Hutchinson, who was prominent in early colonial history, and daughter of Sir John and Elizabeth (Cope) Dryden, was born at Canons Ashby, county of Northampton, England, in the early part of the reign of Queen Elizabeth. In 1589, she married the Rev. Francis Marbury, of Alford, county of Lincoln, son of William and Agnes (Lenton) Marbury, by whom, some say, she had twenty children. The family removed to London about the year 1600, and, upon the death of her husband in that place,

(36)

in 1610–11, she was required, in pursuance of the provisions of his will, "to keep all his said children at her own charge one whole year after his decease if, in the meantime, she did not bestow them in marriage or place them in service."

DESCENT.	Bridget Dryden	married	Francis Marbury;
whose daughter,	Catherine Marbury,	"	Richard Scott;
" son,	John Scott,	"	Rebecca (——) ;
" "	Silvanus Scott,	"	Joanna Jenckes;
" daughter,	Esther "	"	Thomas Sayles;
" son,	John Sayles,	"	Martha Arnold;
" "	Ishmael Sayles,	"	Deborah Aldrich;
" "	Arnold "	"	Lillis Irons;
" daughter,	Deborah "	"	Raymond Burton;
" "	Adaline Burton,	"	John W. Thayer.

Dyer.

MARY DYER was put to death on Boston Common during the Quaker persecution in 1650–62. She and her husband, William, soon after their arrival in this country, joined Rev. John Wilson's church at Boston. When the trouble arose between the Boston church and Rev. John Wheelwright and Ann Hutchinson, Mary and her husband became "notoriously infected with Mrs Hutchinson's errors, and were very censorious and troublesome." They were accordingly banished from the colony, and settled at Newport, R. I. In 1652 Mary returned to England with her husband and remained there five years, her husband coming back to Newport. Upon arriving again at Boston, in 1657, she was put into prison by the authorities for preaching, she having become a minister of the Quaker denomination while abroad. Through the intercession of her husband, who came from Newport to her relief, she was released, but the conditions were—he must take her back to Newport, and under "a heavy penalty not to lodge her in any town of the colony nor to permit any to have speech with her in the journey." She remained away from Boston this time two years.

In 1659 she for the third time visited Boston, and was immediately arrested, tried and condemned to death. She and two others, Marmaduke Stephenson and William Robinson, were led to the scaffold on Boston Common, and the two men were first put to death and their bodies stripped and thrown into a ditch unburied. Her dress was then tied about her feet, the rope was placed about her neck and the noose adjusted. The handkerchief had been placed over her face and the drop was upon the point of being sprung when a cry was heard:

"Stop! she is reprieved" At the last moment, longer unable to withstand the pleadings of her son, Governor Endi-

(38)

cott had relented. Mary took occasion, next day, to address the court in a letter: "Once more to the General Court assembled in Boston speaks Mary Dyer even as before: My life is not accepted, neither availeth me in comparison of the lives and liberty of the truth."

She was again sent back to Newport by the authorities.

In May, 1660, Mary returned to Boston for the last time. Upon being promptly brought before Governor Endicott, he asked:

"Are you the same Mary that was here before?"

"I am the same Mary Dyer," she replied.

"You will own yourself a Quaker, will you not?"

"I own myself to be reproachfully so called."

She was then sentenced to be hung the next day, June 1. From the prison to the gallows she was accompanied by a band of soldiers, and drums were beaten before and behind her that none might hear her speak. On the gallows she was urged by Rev. John Wilson, her first pastor in this country:

"Oh, repent, Mary Dyer, and be not so deluded and carried away by the deceit of the devil."

She was also accused of having said she had been in Paradise, to which she replied:

"Yea, I have been in Paradise these several days. No ear can hear, no tongue can utter, no heart can understand the sweet incomes and the refreshings of the spirit of the Lord which I now feel."

When the death sentence was pronounced, she replied:

"This is no more than what you said before."

"But now it is to be executed, therefore prepare yourself," said Governor Endicott.

Again her dress was tied about her feet, the rope was placed about her neck, and this time the drop fell.

"She did hang as a flag," said one of the judges scoffingly "for others to take example by."

(39)

DYER.

The Friends' records at Portsmouth, R. I., of that date, have the following:

"Mary Dyer, the wife of William Dyer, of Newport, in R. I.; she was put to death at the town of Boston with the like cruel hand as the martyrs were in Queen Mary's time"

Mary Dyer has been described "a person of no mean extract or parentage, of an estate pretty plentiful, of a comely stature and countenance, of a piercing knowledge of many things, and of a wonderful sweet and pleasant discourse."

Governor Winthrop says: "A very promp and fair woman, of a very proud spirit."

The family tradition is that William and Mary Dyer were cousins. George, Edward and Tabitha Dyer, it was said, came from England to Boston in 1627–29, and William, the son of one, and Mary, the daughter of another, married each other.

WILLIAM DYER, whose wife, Mary, was put to death on Boston Common, was a milliner by trade, and came from London, England, to Boston in December, 1635. He and his wife joined Rev. Mr. Wilson's church. Two years later, when the trouble with Rev. John Wheelwright arose, he, with others, signed a remonstrance affirming the innocence of Mr. Wheelwright, and claiming "the court had condemned the truth of Christ." For this he was disfranchised and ordered to deliver up to the authorities all arms, ammunition, etc., in his possession. In 1638 he removed to Portsmouth, R. I., where he was at once elected clerk and signed the civil compact. In 1640 he had settled at Newport, and for eight years acted as secretary for both towns. In 1648 he was chosen general recorder, and from 1650 to 1653, inclusive, he acted as attorney general. During this last period he went to England with Roger Williams and John Clarke to obtain a revocation of Governor Coddington's power. In May, 1653, he was commissioned as "Commander-in-Chief upon sea," to act against the Dutch. In 1654,

DYER.

referring in his report to the alleged encroachments of Governor Coddington upon the highway, he said:

"Let them, therefore, that know any injury in this kind put it down under their hands, as I now have done, and be ready to make it good, as I am, so shall we avoid hypocrisy, dissimulation, backbiting and secret wolfish devourings, one of another, and declare ourselves men, which, how unmanlike, the practice of some sycophants are, is and may be demonstrated. Therefore, let us all that love the light come forth to the light and show their deeds."

In 1661-62 he was appointed commissioner, in 1664-66 deputy, in 1665-66-68 general solicitor, and in 1669 secretary to the council. In 1669 the assembly ordered the execution to proceed in the case brought against him by William Coddington for killing a mare. In 1669 testimony was given by Governor Coddington and others proving his title to Dyer's Island. In 1670 he deeded this island to his son, William. After the death of his wife upon the gallows in 1660, he married Catherine (——), and died in 1677 at Newport.

CHARLES DYER, son of William and Mary (——) Dyer, was born at Newport, R. I., in 1650, and married, for his second wife, Martha (Brownell) Wait, widow of Jeremiah Wait, of Portsmouth, about 1675. He died at Newport, May 15, 1709, and was buried on the Dyer farm, at the extreme end of Old Newport, opposite Coaster's Island, on Narragansett Bay.

CHARLES DYER, son of Charles and Martha (Brownell) Dyer, was born at Newport, R. I., about 1680, and married. August 26, 1709, Mary Lapham, daughter of John and Mary (Mann) Lapham, of Dartmouth, Mass. He was a blacksmith by trade, and for a short time after his marriage lived at Dartmouth, but soon, in 1713, removed to Providence, or "three miles west of salt water," at Mashantatuck (Cranston). He died January 7, 1727, at Cranston, leaving an estate valued at £533.

(41)

DYER.

BETHIAH DYER,* believed to be a daughter of Charles and Mary (Lapham) Dyer, was born at Cranston, R. I., about 1710–20, and married, September 29, 1734, Jeremiah Irons, son of Samuel and Sarah (Whipple) Irons, of Cranston. They removed to Burrillville about 1739, where she probably died.

DESCENT.		Bethiah Dyer	married	Jeremiah Irons;
whose son,		Jeremiah Irons,	"	Barbery Tucker;
"	daughter,	Lillis Irons,	"	Arnold Sayles;
"	"	Deborah Sayles,	"	Raymond Burton;
"	"	Adaline Burton,	"	John W. Thayer.

*See Index.

England.

WILLIAM ENGLAND, one of the early settlers at Portsmouth, R. I., was a resident of that town as early as 1644, when he was granted four acres of land. His wife was Elizabeth (——), whom he married previous to 1640. She survived him and married a second time.

ELEANOR ENGLAND, daughter of William and Elizabeth (——) England, was born at Portsmouth, R. I., about 1645, and July 27, 1665, married Jeremiah Westcott, son of Stukeley Westcott, of Warwick, R. I. She died at Warwick in 1686.

DESCENT.	Eleanor England	married	Jeremiah Westcott;
whose son,	William Westcott,	"	Abigail Gardiner;
" "	Capt. Wm. "	"	Katherine (——);
" daughter,	Alice "	"	Benjamin Burton;
" son,	Edmond Burton,	"	Lucretia Boardman;
" "	Raymond "	"	Deborah Sayles;
" daughter,	Adaline "	"	John W. Thayer.

Francis.

JOHN FRANCIS, one of the early settlers of Braintree, Mass., came not long after the opening of the iron works, in 1645. In 1659, a petition was sent to the General Court from Braintree, "humbly desiring some relief to several persons brought by the owners of the iron works that are likely to be chargeable to them, especially in relation to John Francis, his poor condition calling for present relief." The petition was referred to the next term of the court. His wife, Rose, died during the year. In 1679, the town granted him one hundred acres of land. The date of his death has not been discovered.

DAMARIS FRANCIS, daughter of John and Rose (——) Francis, was born at Braintree, Mass., about 1655, and married Joseph Clark, August 19, 1675. She died, probably, at Braintree.

DESCENT.	Damaris Francis	married	Joseph Clark;
whose son,	Jonathan Clark,	"	Jemima Staples;
" daughter,	Jemima "	"	William Linfield;
" "	Sarah Linfield,	"	Reuben Thayer;
" son,	Caleb Thayer,	"	Patience Phillips;
" "	John W. "	"	Adaline Burton.

Gardiner.

GEORGE GARDINER will live in history, chiefly in the accounts of the suffering endured by his remarkable wife during the religious persecutions of 1658-'60. He was one of the early settlers of Newport, R. I., and was admitted an inhabitant of the island of Aquidneck as far back as 1638. Two years later he had fifty-eight acres of land recorded in his name. In 1641, he was admitted a freeman; in 1642, was constable and senior sergeant; in 1644, ensign, and, in 1662, a commissioner. Upon separating from his first wife, Herodias (Long) Hicks, the cause of which will be found in the sketch of her life, he married again about 1668. In 1673, he was a grand juror, and died at Newport about 1677. In a family Bible, recorded in 1790, is the following memoranda of doubtful authenticity: "Joseph Gardiner, youngest son of Sir Thomas Gardiner, Knight, came over among the first settlers and died in Kings County, Rhode Island State, aged 78 years. Born 1601, died 1679. Left six sons: Benoni, died 1731, aged 104; Henry, died 1737, aged 101; William died at sea by pirates; George lived to see 94 years, and Nicholas and Joseph lived also to a great age.

GEORGE GARDINER, son of George and Herodias (Hicks) Gardiner, was born at Newport, R. I., about 1647, and married Tabitha Tefft, daughter of John and Mary (——) Tefft, of Portsmouth, February 13, 1670. He settled at Kings Town, where he died in 1724.

ABIGAIL GARDINER, daughter, probably, of George and Tabitha (Tefft) Gardiner, was born at Kings Town, R. I., about 1685, and married William Westcott, son of Jeremiah and

(45)

GARDINER.

Eleanor (England) Westcott, of Warwick. They, soon after, removed to Cranston, where she died about 1735, or later.

Descent.			
	Abigail Gardiner	married	William Westcott;
whose son,	Capt. William Westcott, "		Katherine (——);
" daughter,	Alice	" "	Benjamin Burton;
" son,	Edmond Burton,	"	Lucretia Boardman;
" "	Raymond "	"	Deborah Sayles;
" daughter,	Adaline,	" "	John W. Thayer.

Hearnden.

BENJAMIN HEARNDEN came to Providence, R. I., early in its settlement, and, about 1650, married Elizabeth White, daughter of William and Elizabeth (——) White, then of Providence, but later of Boston, Mass. In 1662, upon their removal to Boston, he bought a house and lot of William and Elizabeth White, his wife paying her parents £20 for it. In 1670, a fine imposed upon him by the General Court of Trials was remitted by the Assembly. In 1680, the Assembly again remitted a fine imposed upon his wife, "he pleading his great poverty and the debility of himself and wife." He died in 1687, at Providence.

WILLIAM HEARNDEN, son of Benjamin and Elizabeth (White) Hearnden, was born at Providence, R. I., about 1665, and, about 1685, married Esther (——). She died about 1695, and he married again. He was a shoemaker by trade, and died at Providence, August 27, 1727.

ABIGAIL HEARNDEN, daughter of William and Esther (——) Hearnden, was born at Providence, R. I., about 1695, and married John Tucker, the famous Indian fighter, and son of Morris and Elizabeth (——) Tucker, of Providence. They removed to Burrillville, or Gloucester, where, after his death in 1748, she married Daniel Bartlett, September 25, 1749. She died, probably, at Gloucester.

DESCENT.			
	Abigail Hearnden	married	John Tucker;
whose son,	Morris Tucker,	"	Esther Tower;
" daughter,	Barbery "	"	Jeremiah Irons;
" "	Lillis Irons,	"	Arnold Sayles;
" "	Deborah Sayles,	"	Raymond Burton;
"	Adaline Burton,	"	John W. Thayer.

Hicks.

HERODIAS (LONG) HICKS, wife of George Gardiner, of Newport, R. I., and one of the noted sufferers from the religious persecutions of the Boston church, had a somewhat eventful life before coming under the lash of the Massachusetts executioner. This story can be best told in her own words. In 1665, upon her complaint, her husband, George Gardiner, was before the Rhode Island Assembly. She then testified that when her father died in England, she was sent to London, where she was married, unknown to her friends, to one John Hicks, privately, in the under church of Paul's, called St. Faith's church. She was then 13 or 14 years of age. She came to New England soon after with her husband, and lived at Weymouth, Mass., two years and a half, removing to Rhode Island about 1640. A difference between her and her husband arose soon after, resulting in his going away to the Dutch and taking with him most of her estate, which had been sent her by her mother. After this desertion by John Hicks, she became the wife of George Gardiner, and by him had many children. Testimony was given as to this second marriage by Robert Stanton, who said that "one night, at his house, both of them did say, before him and his wife, that they did take one the other as man and wife." Having lived with her last husband eighteen or twenty years, she now desired of the Assembly that "the estate and labor he had of mine, he may allow it me and the house upon my land I may enjoy without molestation, and that he may allow me my child to bring up, with maintenance for her, and that he be restrained from troubling me more." After this second separation, she married a third husband.

In 1658, while she was still the wife of George Gardiner, she went, with her babe at her breast, "a very sore journey, and, according to man, hardly accomplishable, through a wilderness of above sixty miles," from Newport to Weymouth, to deliver her religious testimony. She was promptly carried to Boston, before Governor John Endicott, who sentenced her to be whipped with ten lashes. Mary Stanton, who came with her to bear her child, also received the same punishment. After the whipping with the three-fold knotted whip of cords, she was continued for fourteen days longer in prison. The narrator concludes: "After the savage, inhuman and bloody execution upon her, of your cruelty, aforesaid, kneeled down and prayed the Lord to forgive you." The date and place of her death can not be given.

DESCENT.	Herodias Hicks	married George Gardiner;
whose son,	George Gardiner,	" Tabitha Tefft;
" daughter,	Abigail "	" William .Westcott;
" son,	Captain Wm. Westcott,	" Katherine (——);
" daughter,	Alice Westcott,	" Benjamin Burton;
" son,	Edmond Burton,	" Lucretia Boardman;
" "	Raymond "	" Deborah Sayles;
" daughter,	Adaline "	" John W. Thayer.

Holbrook.

THOMAS HOLBROOK, of Broadway, England, was probably one of the party who followed their pastor, the Rev. Mr. Barnard, from Weymouth, Dorsetshire, England, and settled at Weymouth, Mass., giving that name to the place previously known as Wessagusset. He sailed from Weymouth, England, March 20, 1635-6, and located in the northern part of the town near tide water, on what has long since borne the name of "Old Spain." His name first appears on the records in America in 1640. He arranged to move to Rehoboth in 1644, but for some reason did not, thereby forfeiting his lot there. He was six times chosen selectman from 1641 to 1654, in the latter year removing to Dorchester. In 1668 he had removed to Medfield, where he died in 1677, age 76 years. In his will he gave his sword to one grandchild, his gun to another, and his musket to a third.

His sons were requested, in regard to their mother, "to be helpful to her in all ways as she is ancient and weak of body." To his son, John, he gave a double share of the estate.

His wife, Jane; son, John, and three other children, came over from England with him. She was then thirty-four.

CAPTAIN JOHN HOLBROOK, son of Thomas and Jane (——) Holbrook, was born at Broadway, England, in 1617, and came to America with his father in 1624, from Weymouth, Dorsetshire. He married Sarah (——), and settled at Weymouth. She died January 14, 1643-4. For his second wife he married Elizabeth Stream, daughter of Elizabeth Stream, a widow. He lived in that part of Weymouth known as "Old Spain." In 1648 he was chosen selectman, and from 1651 to 1673, he was six times chosen representative. He was an enterprising business man and a large holder of real estate, owning land in Scituate and

(50)

HOLBROOK.

Braintree as well as at Weymouth. He also owned a house in Boston. In Braintree he owned the eastern portion, about 600 acres, of the tract of 3,000 acres granted by Boston in January, 1644, to the "Company of Undertakers for the Iron Works." In 1681 the new school-house was built on land bought of him at Braintree. He was prominent in military affairs, and active during the King Philip war. In 1664, as lieutenant of the local company, he was chosen to go upon some service in Captain Hudson's command, but sickness in his family prevented. In the spring of 1676 he was appointed captain of one of the companies raised and sent out to suppress the "insolencies" of the Indians, and "to range the woods towards Hassanamesit" (above the Merrimac). In a report to his superiors, made April 29, 1676, he complained that his company was not up to the quota, and unless the ranks could be filled, he asked to be dismissed. "I have neither drume nor collors which I desire that if you think it fitt to send me either houe-boye or drumpiter which is very requisitt." His second wife died June 25, 1688, and he then married Mary Loring, who survived him. He died at Weymouth, November 23, 1699, leaving a large estate to his numerous heirs.

EUNICE HOLBROOK, daughter of Captain John and Elizabeth (Stream) Holbrook, and one of a pair of twins, was born at Weymouth, Mass., May 12, 1658. She married Benjamin Ludden, son of James and Alice (——) Ludden, of Weymouth, and probably died in the same town.

DESCENT.	Eunice Holbrook	married	Benjamin Ludden;
whose son,	Benjamin Ludden,	"	Sarah (——);
" daughter,	Eunice "	"	Joseph Thayer;
" son,	Reuben Thayer,	"	Sarah Linfield;
" "	Caleb "	"	Patience Phillips;
" "	John W. "	"	Adaline Burton.

(51)

Hopkins.

WILLIAM HOPKINS lived at Cheselborne, England, and about 1600 married Joanna Arnold, daughter of Thomas and Alice (Gulley) Arnold, of the same town.

FRANCES HOPKINS, daughter of William and Joanna (Arnold) Hopkins, was born at Cheselborne, England, in 1614, and married William Mann, of Dorset, or, possibly, Kent County. They came to this country by 1640, or earlier, and settled at Providence, R. I. Upon the death of her husband, in 1650, she went to the home of her son-in-law, John Lapham, at Dartmouth, Mass., where she died February 26, 1700.

DESCENT.		Frances Hopkins	married	William Mann;
whose	daughter,	Mary Mann,	"	John Lapham;
"	"	" Lapham,	"	Charles Dyer;
"	"	Bethiah Dyer,	"	Jeremiah Irons;
"	son,	Jeremiah Irons,	"	Barbery Tucker;
"	daughter,	Lillis Irons,	"	Arnold Sayles;
"	"	Deborah Sayles,	"	Raymond Burton;
"	"	Adaline Burton,	"	John W. Thayer.

Ibrook.

RICHARD IBROOK came from England, probably from the parish of Hingham, in Norfolk County, early in the settlement of the Massachusetts colony, and located at Hingham, on Broad Cove Street. His family consisted of his wife and three daughters. In 1644, he, with several others, became involved in trouble over the election of a commander of a local military company. He was arrested, with several others, and, stoutly refusing to give bail, was sent to jail. After a long and wearisome trial, they were fined different amounts. In 1638, he was also fined for immoral conduct. During the King Philip war, while many fled to the more thickly settled towns, others remained in the Ibrook house, which was fortified to resist the Indian attacks. He died at Hingham, November 14, 1651, his wife dying April 4, 1664.

MARGARET IBROOK, daughter of Richard Ibrook, was born in 1617, probably at Hingham, Norfolk County, England, and, coming to this country with her father, married, at Charlestown, John Tower, son of Robert and Dorothy (Damon) Tower, of Hingham, Mass., February 13, 1638-9. She died at Hingham, May 15, 1700.

	DESCENT.	Margaret Ibrook	married	John Tower;
whose	son,	Ibrook Tower,	"	Margaret Hardin;
"	daughter,	Esther "	"	Morris Tucker;
"	"	Barbery Tucker,	"	Jeremiah Irons;
"	"	Lillis Irons,	"	Arnold Sayles;
"	'	Deborah Sayles,	"	Raymond Burton;
"	"	Adaline Burton,	"	John W. Thayer.

(53)

Inman.

EDWARD INMAN, one of the large land owners in the early settlement of northern Rhode Island, first settled in Warwick, upon coming to this country. This was in 1648. Three years later he moved to Providence, where a small piece of land was granted him to build upon. In 1653 he was found not liable to forfeit his home lot for not building upon it, "because he hath built in another more convenient place for his trade of dressing fox gloves." He is twice recorded as having "entered two ankers of rum." In 1666 he and John Mowry bought 2,000 acres of land, the deed being confirmed by Philip, ten miles north of Providence, near the Pawtucket river, "to have and to hold without any trouble or molestation by any Indians." This section, where he and others soon settled, is now the town of Smithfield. In 1682 the town of Providence, "being inclined to part some of the right," gave them a grant of the land "so a neighborly amity might be settled rather than to use extremity by which animosities might arise." In 1686 he deeded Joshua Clark sixty-six acres, the consideration being "for that said Clark married the daughter of my now wife and for the propagation of a neighborhood." In 1688 he added to his tax list this appeal: "I pray consider our condition, for you have formerly." His list was passed "to be heard." He was eight times appointed deputy, besides holding other public offices. He died at Smithfield in 1706.

His first wife died previous to 1686, and he then married Barbara Phillips, of Smithfield, widow of Michael Phillips. She died soon after the death of her second husband in 1706.

JOANNA INMAN, daughter of Edward and (——) Inman, was born probably at Warwick, R. I., about 1648, and in 1666 married Nathaniel Mowry, son of Roger and Mary (——)

(54)

INMAN.

Mowry, of Smithfield, to which place her father had removed. Her husband, who died in 1718, she survived.

Descent.		Joanna Inman	married	Nathaniel Mowry;
whose daughter,	Mary Mowry,		"	John Arnold;
"	son,	William Arnold,	"	Hannah Whipple;
"	daughter,	Martha "	"	John Sayles;
"	son,	Ishmael Sayles,	"	Deborah Aldrich;
"	"	Arnold "	"	Lillis Irons;
"	daughter,	Deborah "	"	Raymond Burton;
"	"	Adaline Burton,	"	John W. Thayer.

Irons.

MATTHEW IRONS, one of the early settlers of New England, came to this country about 1630, and was admitted to the Boston church, April 20, 1634. He was at that time in the employ of William Colborn. In 1636, he was admitted freeman, but being a supporter of Wheelwright he was disarmed in 1637. He was not exiled, however, as were Wheelwright's more prominent sympathizers. In 1657, he petitioned the General Court to remit a fine of £5 imposed upon him "for suffering a man to be drunk and not sending for a constable as the law requires." His petition was refused. His wife was Ann (——). Both probably died at Boston. By his will, dated January 30, 1661, he gave his fowling piece to one son, and his musket and sword to another.

SAMUEL IRONS, son of Matthew and Ann (——) Irons, was born at Boston, Mass., November 24, 1650, and married Sarah Belcher, daughter of John and Sarah (——) Belcher, of Braintree, November 13, 1677. He settled at Braintree, and probably died there.

SAMUEL IRONS, son of Samuel and Sarah (Belcher) Irons, was born at Braintree, Mass., about 1685, and married Sarah Whipple, daughter of Jonathan and Margaret (Angell) Whipple, of Providence, R. I., May 3, 1709. He was a tailor by trade, and settled at Cranston, where he died December 31, 1720.

JEREMIAH IRONS, son of Samuel and Sarah (Whipple) Irons, was born, probably, at Cranston, R. I., November 29, 1711, and married, it is believed, Bethiah Dyer, daughter of

IRONS.

Charles and Mary (Lapham) Dyer, of Cranston, September 29, 1734. About 1739, they removed to Burrillville, where he probably died.

CAPTAIN JEREMIAH IRONS, son of Jeremiah and Bethiah (Dyer) Irons, was born at Burrillville, R. I., in 1748, and married Barbery Tucker, daughter of Morris and Esther (Tower) Tucker, of Burrillville. In personal appearance he was small in stature and cross-eyed; in disposition, quick-tempered, and, in his actions, energetic. In the government of his children he completely failed to exert any restraining influence, but when driven to it made use of his most potential threat, "Stop, children, or I will tell your mother." Harmless as this threat might seem, it usually had the desired effect; why is explained in the sketch of his wife. He was full of fun, and in his old age retold the same story time and again, oblivious of its previous repetition. He invariably carried a cane and had a habit of trotting his foot over his knee. Before his death, his constant companion for years, and until she grew up, had been his granddaughter, Sarah A. Trescott. They slept together till she was fourteen years of age, and, towards each other, they were like brother and sister. He was immersed after he was ninety years of age as the result of his conversion during a religious revival. During the Revolutionary war he served, most of the time, in Captain Stephen Winsor's company, Colonel Brown's regiment of the Rhode Island militia. He enlisted from Gloucester in October, 1776, and was dis-·harged, finally, sometime in 1781, having served at different periods, two months as private, six months and twenty days as sergeant, two months as ensign, and two months as lieutenant. He was under arms in readiness to take part in the battle of Rhode Island, August 29, 1778, but finally was not called into the engagement. He applied for a pension from Burrillville, August 7, 1832, at the age of 83. The pension was granted. He died at Burrillville, May 5, 1842, and his grave, in 1894,

IRONS.

was located in the back part of the old burying ground on the "Plains," between Chepachet and Mapleville.

LILLIS IRONS, daughter of Captain Jeremiah and Barbery (Tucker) Irons, was born at Burrillville, R. I., in April, 1776, and, February 27, 1795, married Arnold Sayles, son of Ishmael and Deborah (Aldrich) Sayles, of Burrillville. They afterwards moved to Chepachet. In her younger days she was considered handsome, and proved a very neat and energetic housekeeper. She was the mother of thirteen children, and the cares of such a family confined her closely to the house during the day. In the evening, however, she was a "great hand" to go visiting, frequently leaving the younger ones in care of one of the older children while she was at the neighbors'. The writer remembers her as she appeared a short time before her death. She was then living in Chepachet, "down on the Point," in the last house on the north side of the road. The morning he visited her she was sitting by the fire, a little woman, considerably bent, and smoking a pipe. She died August 20, 1865, a little less than 90 years of age, and lies buried in the back part of the old burying ground, on the "Plains," between Chepachet and Mapleville.

DESCENT.	Lillis Irons	married	Arnold Sayles;
whose daughter,	Deborah Sayles,	"	Raymond Burton;
" "	Adaline Burton,	"	John W. Thayer.

Jenckes.

JOSEPH JENCKES, the builder of the first fire engine used in Boston and, probably, in America, was born in 1602, at Hammersmith, or Hounslow, or at Colnbrook, in the edge of Bucks, near London. The names of his ancestors have been traced back through ten generations to Robert Jenks, of Wolverton (Manor), in the parish of Eaton-under-Eywood, Shropeshire, to the reign of Edward III., in 1350. Robert was the son of Jenkyn Cansbrey, of Wolverton, and of Dorothy, daughter and coheiress of Sir Walter Collyng, Knight of Church Stretton, in the same county. From Robert the ancestry is traceable as far back as Welch annals and bardic pedigree are carried in the house of Elystan Glodrydd.

Joseph Jenckes came to this country with his son, Joseph, early in the settlement of the Massachusetts colony, and in 1645 had settled at Lynn. He was then a widower. He was by trade a blacksmith, and was one of the workmen whom John Winthrop, the younger, engaged and brought over with him in order to start the iron foundry at Lynn. In 1646, June 10, he was granted "liberty to make experience of his ability and inventions for ye making of engines for mills to go with water for the more speedy despatch of work than formerly and mills for the making of scythes and edge tools with a new invented saw mill, that things may be afforded cheaper than formerly." This petition was granted for fourteen years "without disturbance by any other setting up like inventions that so his study and costs may not be in vain or lost." He soon became known as the "patentee," his patents being among the earliest taken out in the country. He made the dies for coining the first money used in the colony, was the first founder who worked in brass and iron, and by his hands the first models were made and the first castings taken of many domestic implements and iron tools.

JENCKES.

The first article said to have been cast was a small iron pot, since in possession of the late Alonzo Lewis, historian of Lynn. That he built the first fire engines used in Boston is seen from the extract: "Boston Town Records—12th, 1, 1653-4. At a meeting this day * * * the selectmen have power and liberty to agree with Joseph Jynks for Ingins to Carry water in Case of fire if they see Cause soe to doe." In 1666, November 29, he was admonished by the court for not attending public worship.

His second wife was Elizabeth (——), whom he married at Lynn, in 1646. She died in July, 1679, at Providence, R I., to which place they had removed late in life, first stopping at Warwick for a time. He died in March, 1683, at Providence.

JOSEPH JENCKES, son of Joseph Jenckes, was born near London, England, in 1632. When his father came to this country, in 1643, the lad was left by him with his maternal grandparents, his own mother being dead. His father assigned a sum of money sufficient for his maintenance till he should become of age, when he was to join his father in America. He crossed the seas, however, at the age of 16, and came to his father at Lynn, Mass., where he married Esther Ballard, daughter of William and Elizabeth (——) Ballard. In 1661, in May, he was accused before the General Court of high misdemeanors in divers treasonable words against the King's majesty. He was acquitted, however. In 1669 he removed to Warwick, R. I., where he built a saw mill on the Pawtuxet river, agreeing, when he purchased the privilege from the owners, to let them have boards at 4 shillings 6 pence "the hundred," and all other "sawn work" at the same rate. In January, 1670, he served as foreman of a jury in the case of a man and wife "who were both drowned in the river of Pawtuxet the 16th at night." In 1671 he built a forge and saw mill at Pawtucket Falls, which was destroyed by fire five years later by the Indians in the King Philip war. In 1680 he and two others were empowered to

JENCKES.

purchase a bell for the use of the colony to give notice of the sittings of the Assembly, Courts of Trial and General Council. Earlier the members of the Assembly were called together by beat of drum. In January, 1690, he and five others wrote to William and Mary, among other things, congratulating them upon their accession to the throne. He was three times chosen deputy and served as assistant thirteen years. He died at Providence, January 4, 1717.

JOANNA JENCKES, daughter of Joseph and Esther (Ballard) Jenckes, was born at Warwick, R. I., in 1672, and married Silvanus Scott, son of John and Rebecca (——) Scott, of Providence, about 1692 They moved to Smithfield in 1695, where she died, March 12, 1756, leaving an estate, derived from her deceased husband fourteen years before, of £2,214.

DESCENT.	Joanna Jenckes married Silvanus Scott;		
whose daughter,	Esther Scott,	"	Thomas Sayles;
" son,	John Sayles,	"	Martha Arnold;
" "	Ishmael "	"	Deborah Aldrich;
" "	Arnold "	"	Lillis Irons;
" daughter,	Deborah "	"	Raymond Burton;
" "	Adaline Burton,	"	John W. Thayer.

(61)

Johnson.

JOHN JOHNSON'S name was made famous one morning in February, 1645, at Roxbury, Mass., by the seventeen barrels of powder stored in his house blowing it to atoms. He was the "surveyor-general of all ye armyes," and, when Ann Hutchinson was taken into custody because of her religious opinions, the General Court ordered that the arms and ammunition of all her Roxbury adherents should be delivered into the custody of John Johnson. This was in 1637, and Governor Winthrop has described what followed: "John Johnson, having built a fair house in the midst of the town, with divers barns and other out-buildings, it fell on fire (February 6, 1645) in the day-time (no man knowing by what occasion), and there being in it seventeen barrels of the country's powder and many arms, all was suddenly burnt and blown up to the value of £400 or £500. Wherein a special providence of God appeared, for he being from home, the people came together to help and many were in the house, no man thinking of the powder till one of the company put them in mind of it whereupon they all withdrew and soon after the powder took fire and blew up all about it and shook the houses in Boston and Cambridge so as men thought it had been an earthquake and carried great pieces of timber a good way off and some rags and such light things beyond Boston meeting house."

John Johnson came to America in the "Arabella," in 1630, with Governor Winthrop's party, from Groton, Suffolk County, England. He settled at Roxbury, where he was soon appointed constable, and in 1631 was admitted freeman. In 1639, having paid ten shillings to the company, he was "freed from training." In 1640 he was "freed from training without any pay," because of his other services. He kept a tavern on Roxbury street, where many public meetings were held, and

JOHNSON.

" was a very industrious and faithful man in his place." He represented Roxbury in the General Court fourteen years, and was a member of the church when it was first organized. He died September 29, 1659, at Roxbury. His wife was Margery (——). His homestead was on the southwest corner of Washington and Ball streets, Boston, then Roxbury.

MARY JOHNSON, daughter of John and Margery (——·) Johnson, was born at Groton, Suffolk County, England, and, coming to America with her father in 1630, married Roger Mowry, a "kinsman" of Roger Williams, of Salem, Mass., about 1635. They removed to Providence, R. I., about 1643. After the death, in 1666, of her husband, she married John Kingsley, in 1674, and died at Rehoboth, Mass., January 29, 1679.

DESCENT.   Mary Johnson   married Roger Mowry;
whose daughter, Hannah Mowry,   "   Benjamin Sherman;
"   "   Deborah Sherman, "   Elisha Johnson;
" son,   Ebenezer Johnson, "   Elizabeth Tingley;
" daughter, Catherine   "   "   Thomas Phillips;
"   "   Patience Phillips, "   Caleb Thayer;
" son,   John W. Thayer,   "   Adaline Burton

Johnson.

JOHN JOHNSON, of Westerly, R. I., previous to settling in that place, probably came from Rehoboth, Mass. His wife was Mary (——), and he died at Westerly, in 1702.

JOHN JOHNSON, son of John and Mary (——) Johnson, was born at Rehoboth, Mass., about 1670, and removed with his father to Westerly, R. I., where he died in 1733. His wife, Elizabeth (——), survived him.

ELISHA JOHNSON, son of John and Elizabeth (——) Johnson, was probably born at Westerly, R. I., about 1690. He married Deborah Sherman, daughter of Benjamin and Hannah (Mowry) Sherman, of Portsmouth. He then removed to Coventry. For his second wife he married Deborah Yeats, of East Greenwich, July 9, 1750. He died at Coventry, in July, 1774, leaving to his son, Ebenezer, " the sum of six shillings, lawful money."

EBENEZER JOHNSON, son of Elisha and Deborah (Sherman) Johnson, was born at Coventry, R. I., in 1734, and married Elizabeth Tingley, daughter of Ephraim and Hannah (——) Tingley, of Coventry, about 1760.

He was a man of large frame and very active about his trade, which was that of gun and blacksmith. The writer has in his possession a little, short-stemmed iron pipe made by Ebenezer in his gunshop. This pipe was frequently brought into use by him during his working hours. It was his ambition, during his later days, to live to be 100 years old, and he frequently announced he would indulge himself in a turkey dinner on the 100th anniversary of his birth. A short time before he died he walked from his house to the factory at Washington,

(64)

JOHNSON.

a mile distant. Eleven days before the date which was the goal of his ambition he died, in the year 1834. He was buried in Mapleroot cemetery.

CATHERINE JOHNSON, daughter of Ebenezer and Elizabeth (Tingley) Johnson, was born at Coventry, R. I., in 1771, and married Thomas Phillips, son of James Phillips, of Coventry, in 1788. They settled at Sterling, Conn., and lived there many years. She died at Jewett City, Conn., where she was buried. It is said she had an even, pleasant disposition, and never made an enemy.

DESCENT. Catherine Johnson married Thomas Phillips;
whose daughter, Patience Phillips, " Caleb Thayer;
" son, John W. Thayer, " Adaline Burton.

Knowles.

HENRY KNOWLES, one of the early settlers of Portsmouth, R. I., was born in England, January 6, 1609, and, after living at Portsmouth till 1655, he moved to Warwick. In 1657, an action of trespass was there brought against him. In Portsmouth, he had also been ordered "to cut his lot shorter." In 1664, with three others, he was authorized by the town "to keep Ordinaries for the entertainment of strangers" during the session of the King's Court at Warwick. In 1666, he, with other members of a coroner's jury, found the following somewhat ambiguous verdict:

"We, who are engaged to see this dead Indian, do find, by diligent search, that he was beaten, which was the cause of his death."

Henry Knowles died at Kings Town, in January, 1670. His wife, who was the daughter of Robert Potter, of Portsmouth, survived him.

MARY KNOWLES, daughter of Henry and (——) Knowles, was born at Portsmouth, R. I., and came to Warwick with her father in 1655. She married Moses Lippitt, son of John and (——) Lippitt, of Warwick, November 19, 1668, and died at ˙Varwick, December 28, 1719.

DESCENT.	Mary Knowles	married	Moses Lippitt;
whose daughter,	Martha Lippitt,	"	Thomas Burlingame;
" "	Persis Burlingame,	"	William Burton;
" son,	Benjamin Burton,	"	Alice Westcott;
" "	Edmond "	"	Lucretia Boardman;
" "	Raymond "	"	Deborah Sayles;
" daughter,	Adaline "	"	John W. Thayer.

(66)

Lapham.

THOMAS LAPHAM came to this country from Tenterden, County of Kent, England, about 1630, and settled at Scituate, Mass., where he probably died.

JOHN LAPHAM, son of Thomas Lapham, was born at Scituate, Mass., in 1635, and April 6, 1673, married Mary Mann, daughter of William and Frances (Hopkins) Mann, of Providence, where he soon settled. In the same year he was appointed deputy, and two years later was chosen constable. During the King Philip war, his house was burned by the Indians. In 1680, he had removed to Newport, and two years later to Dartmouth, Mass. In 1699, at a meeting held at his house, he contributed £5 towards a "meeting house for the people of God, in scorn called Quakers, 35 foot long, 30 foot wide and 14 foot stud." It was the first Quaker meeting house in Dartmouth. He died at Dartmouth, in April, 1710, leaving an estate of £362, including land at Providence as well as Dartmouth.

MARY LAPHAM, daughter of John and Mary (Mann) Lapham, was born at Dartmouth, Mass., October 5, 1686, and married, August 26, 1709, Charles Dyer, son of Charles and Martha (Brownell) Dyer, of Newport, R. I. They removed to Cranston, where she died in 1735 or later.

DESCENT.	Mary Lapham	married	Charles Dyer;
whose daughter,	Bethiah Dyer,	"	Jeremiah Irons;
" son,	Jeremiah Irons,	"	Barbery Tucker;
" daughter,	Lillis Irons,	"	Arnold Sayles;
" "	Deborah Sayles,	"	Raymond Burton;
" "	Adaline Burton,	"	John W. Thayer.

Linfield.

WILLIAM LINFIELD, probably the first of the family name to settle in this country, was, for many years, a resident of Braintree, Mass. In 1697, he, with several others, agreed in writing to defend the title to their lands by paying the costs of litigation begun by Boston parties who laid claim to the property. He probably died at Braintree. His wife was Abigail (——).

WILLIAM LINFIELD, son of William and Abigail (——) Linfield, was born at Braintree, Mass., December 5, 1694, and married, August 14, 1718, Elizabeth Littlefield, daughter of Edmond and Elizabeth (Mott) Littlefield, of Braintree. In 1730 he was chosen constable, but refused to serve, and accordingly was obliged to pay £5 to the town treasurer. He was also chosen fence viewer in 1735, fire warden in 1752, and hogreeve and town surveyor at other times. He died at Braintree in 1785.

WILLIAM LINFIELD, son of William and Elizabeth (Littlefield) Linfield, was born at Braintree, Mass., December 10, 1718, and married Jemima Clark, daughter of Jonathan and Jemima (Staples) Clark, of Braintree, about 1742. In April, 1775, during the Revolutionary war, he was under arms four days. In March, 1776, he was called out for fifteen days. In June, the same year, he served four days, and in August, 1778, he was mustered in for thirteen days. He died at Braintree, March 2, 1807.

SARAH LINFIELD, daughter of William and Jemima (Clark) Linfield, was born at Braintree, Mass., about 1743, and, September 17, 1768, married Reuben Thayer, son of Joseph and

LINFIELD.

Eunice (Ludden) Thayer, of Randolph. They lived at Randolph till late in life, when they moved to Sterling, Conn , where she died October 28, 1813.

DESCENT. Sarah Linfield   married Reuben Thayer;
whose son,   Caleb Thayer,   "   Patience Phillips;
"   "   John W. Thayer,   "   Adaline Burton.

Lippitt.

JOHN LIPPITT, one of the early settlers at Providence, R. I., came from England as early as 1638, in which year he had a lot and six acres of land at Providence. In 1647 he was chosen one of the commissioners to meet at Portsmouth to form a government under the charter. In 1648 he had removed to Warwick, where he was living as late as 1669. He probably died soon after. Nothing is known of his wife.

MOSES LIPPITT, son of John and (——) Lippitt, was born at Providence, R. I., or possibly at Warwick, where, November 19, 1668, he married Mary Knowles, daughter of Henry and (——) Knowles, of Warwick. He was, by trade, a tanner. He was five times appointed deputy from 1681 to 1699, was overseer of the poor in 1687, and when he died, January 6, 1703, at Warwick, he left an estate valued at £456, including stock of leather, green hides and bark, tanning instruments, book debts valued at £100, etc. The Lippitt burial ground, in which are still to be found the uninscribed graves of Moses, and doubtless his father as well, is situated in a pasture southeast of the road and a quarter of a mile east of the Quaker meeting house at Old Warwick.

MARTHA LIPPITT, daughter of Moses and Mary (Knowles) Lippitt, was born at Warwick, R. I., about 1670, and married Thomas Burlingame, of Providence, son of Roger and Mary (——) Burlingame, about 1687. They settled at Cranston, where she died in 1723.

DESCENT.	Martha Lippitt	married	Thomas Burlingame;
whose daughter,	Persis Burlingame,	"	William Burton;
" son,	Benjamin Burton,	"	Alice Westcott;
" "	Edmond "	"	Lucretia Boardman;
" "	Raymond "	"	Deborah Sayles;
" daughter,	Adaline "	"	John W. Thayer.

(70)

Littlefield.

EDMOND LITTLEFIELD, one of the prominent supporters of the Rev. John Wheelwright during his troubles with the Boston church, was born in Exeter, England, in 1591, and came to America with his oldest son in 1637. He first settled at Exeter, Mass., but, on account of his religious and political views, being a zealous churchman and Royalist, he was not permitted to remain, and removed, about 1645, to Wells, Maine, where he became a man of considerable distinction. The records show, however, that during some heated religious meeting he so far forgot himself as to put a ballot into the box by proxy for one of his sons against his consent, for which offense he was "presented" at court. It also seems he was for a time licensed to sell liquor, but was cautioned not to sell to any one Indian more than a pint at one time under any pretense whatsoever. In May, 1638, the next year after his arrival at Boston, his wife, Annie, and their six children, followed him to this country, sailing in the ship "Bevis," of Hampton, Captain Tounes. Edmond Littlefield, known as "Old Edmond," to distinguish him from his grandson, Edmond, died at Wells, December 11, 1661, leaving an estate valued at £588.

FRANCIS LITTLEFIELD, son of Edmond and Annie (———) Littlefield, was born at Exeter, England, in 1619. While yet a mere boy, he left home, and for many years his parents lost all trace of him. A short time, however, after their arrival in this country, he reappeared, having in some undiscovered manner crossed the seas ahead of them. When his father was driven from Exeter, Francis went to Woburn, where he married Jane (———). She died, however, soon after, December 20, 1646. He then followed his father to Wells, Maine, where, in 1648, he married Rebecca (———). He, too, kept a public house and continued to sell liquor after the expiration of his license, in

(71)

LITTLEFIELD.

violation of law. He represented Dover in the General Court in 1648, York in 1668, and Wells in 1665 and 1676. He was a strong supporter of the claims of Massachusetts, and the General Court frequently met at his house. He died in 1712, at the advanced age of 93 years. A curious state of affairs existed in his father's family from the fact that there were two sons, each named Francis. This was occasioned by the supposition on the part of his parents, when the elder Francis disappeared years before, that he must be dead, and, acting upon that belief, they named their next born son in remembrance of their lost boy.

EDMOND LITTLEFIELD, " Jr.," son of Francis and Rebecca (——) Littlefield, was born at Wells, Maine, about 1650. In 1680, after the close of the King Philip war, he was granted 200 acres of land with water privilege, as an inducement to build a saw-mill upon the Kennebunk river. He decided, however, not to build, and soon after sold out to other parties. It is thought he then removed to Braintree, Mass., where, about 1685, he married Elizabeth Mott, daughter of Nathaniel and Anna (Shooter) Mott. In 1700, he, with two others, was appointed to "run" the town line. In 1707, he is on record as voting against buying school land. The next year he was ordered to collect the rates, which service would be accepted in place of his serving as constable. He died at Braintree May 27, 1717.

ELIZABETH LITTLEFIELD, daughter of Edmond and Elizabeth (Mott) Littlefield, was born at Braintree, Mass., April 21, 1694, and married William Linfield, son of William and Abigail (——) Linfield, of Braintree, August 14, 1718. She lived, and doubtless died, at Braintree.

DESCENT.	Elizabeth Littlefield married William Linfield;
whose son,	William Linfield, " Jemima Clark;
" daughter, Sarah "	" Reuben Thayer;
" son, Caleb Thayer,	" Patience Phillips;
" " John W. Thayer,	" Adaline Burton.

(72)

Ludden.

JAMES LUDDEN, once called upon to act as a guide for Governor Winthrop through the wilderness, was born in England, in 1611, and was possibly one of the party from Weymouth, Dorsetshire, England, to settle in Weymouth, Mass., in 1624. He was certainly living there in 1632, when the birth of one of his children is recorded. He is believed to have been the guide who piloted Governor Winthrop through the town on his journey a-foot in October, 1632, from Plymouth to Weymouth, a ford on North river being named by the governor "Ludden," in honor of his guide. He was an owner of considerable land in Weymouth, and his name is attached as witness to the deed given by the Indians in 1642 of land now covering a good share of the territory of the town. In 1685 he made affidavit to the execution of this deed, having then lived to a ripe old age. His wife, Alice (——), he probably married in England before coming to this country. He died at Weymouth, February 7, 1692.

BENJAMIN LUDDEN, son of James and Alice (——) Ludden, was born in Weymouth, Mass., January 12, 1656, and married Eunice Holbrook, daughter of John and Elizabeth (Stream) Holbrook, of Weymouth, about 1675. In 1690 he was killed in the French-Indian war during the expedition into Canada under Sir William Phipps. His will, dated July 15, 1690, began as follows:

"Being called forth as a soldier in this time of great distress for to fight the Lord's Battels against the bloudy enemies of the church and the people of God in New England, namely those anti-christians and bloudy french together with their bloudy martherous and salvage Indians, and considering whether I may return again with my life to see my parents, wife and relations, I commit my soul to God," etc.

LUDDEN.

BENJAMIN LUDDEN, son of Benjamin and Eunice (Holbrook) Ludden, was born at Weymouth, March 13, 1681, and married Sarah (——), October 28, 1704. He settled at Braintree. In 1729 he was one of a committee to grant applications for the taking of stone off the common for building purposes. The same year he was on the committee to agree upon some method for dividing the town. He probably died at Braintree.

EUNICE LUDDEN, daughter of Benjamin and Sarah (——) Ludden, was born probably at Braintree, Mass., August 22, 1709. She married Joseph Thayer, of Braintree, son of Ephraim and Sarah (Bass) Thayer, November 16, 1738, and lived in Braintree many years. In 1752 they moved to Randolph, where she died.

DESCENT.	Eunice Ludden	married	Joseph Thayer;
whose son,	Reuben Thayer,	"	Sarah Linfield;
" "	Caleb "	"	Patience Phillips;
" "	John W. "	"	Adaline Burton.

Mann.

WILLIAM MANN, probably from Dorset or Kent County, England, had come to this country and settled at Providence, R. I., with his wife, Frances Hopkins, daughter of William and Joanna (Arnold) Hopkins, of Cheselbourne, Dorset County, as early as 1640. In 1641 he and twelve others complained in a letter to Massachusetts of the "insolent and riotous carriages of Samuel Gorton and his company," and petitioned the authorities to "lend us a neighbor-like, helping hand." He died about 1650 at Providence.

MARY MANN, daughter of William and Frances (Hopkins) Mann, was born probably at Providence, R. I., and married, April 6, 1673, John Lapham, son of Thomas Lapham, of Scituate, Mass. They lived for a time at Providence, and for two years, 1680-2, at Newport, settling finally at Dartmouth, Mass., where she died about 1710.

DESCENT.   Mary Mann married John Lapham;
whose daughter,   "   Lapham,   "   Charles Dyer;
"   "   Bethiah Dyer,   "   Jeremiah Irons;
"   son,   Jeremiah Irons,   "   Barbery Tucker;
"   daughter, Lillis   "   "   Arnold Sayles;
"   "   Deborah Sayles, "   Raymond Burton;
'   Adaline Burton, "   John W. Thayer.

Marbury.

Rev. Francis Marbury, of London, father of Ann Hutchinson, a noted personage in the early colonial history of New England, was born in Grisby, in the parish of Burgh-upon-Bain, in the county of Lincoln, England. He was the son of William Marbury, Esquire, and Agnes, daughter of John Lenton, Esquire. He first married Elizabeth Moore, at St. Peter's at Gowts, in the city of Lincoln, August 19, 1583, by whom he had three daughters. He is described upon the church register as a "gentleman." Soon after the birth of his last child his wife died, and, in 1589, he married, for his second wife, Bridget Dryden, daughter of Sir John and Elizabeth (Cope) Dryden, of Canons Ashby, county of Northampton. About the year 1600 he had moved to London, for, October 28, 1605, he was presented to the rectory at St. Martins-in-the-Vintrey. In 1607-8, February 29, he was presented to the rectory of St. Pancreas, Soper Lane, which position, however, he resigned two years later. Soon after, January 15, 1609-10, he was presented to the rectory of St. Margaret, New Fish street, which position, in conjunction with that at St. Martins-in-the-Vintrey, he held till his death in 1610-11. By his will he bequeathed to his children £1,600. It will be seen, therefore, that Ann Hutchinson and her sister, Catherine, by both parents, were descended from gentle and heraldic families of England.

Catherine Marbury, one of the sufferers from the Quaker persecutions in Boston, was the daughter of the Rev. Francis and Bridget (Dryden) Marbury, and was born in London, England, in 1607. She married Richard Scott, son of Richard and Margaret (Haney) Scott, of Glemsford, county of

MARBURY.

Suffolk, probably on the eve of his departure for America, in 1634. They sailed in the ship "Griffin," and among the passengers was her sister, Ann Hutchinson, afterwards a noted personage in the early colonial history of New England. They lived for a time at Ipswich, Mass., and, in 1637, settled at Providence, R. I.

Governor Winthrop, of Massachusetts, in writing of the spread of Anabaptistry, January 16, 1639, said: "At Providence things grew still worse, for a sister of Mrs. Hutchinson, the wife of one Scott, being affected with Anabaptistry, and going to live at Providence, Mr. Williams was taken (or rather emboldened) by her to make open profession thereof, and accordingly was re-baptized by one Holyman, a poor man, late of Salem. Then Mr. Williams re-baptized him and some ten more."

During the period of the persecution of the Quakers, September 16, 1658, Mrs. Scott's future son-in-law, Christopher Holden, had his right ear cut off at Boston for the crime of being a Quaker, and she was present when the punishment was inflicted. She is described as follows:

"A mother of many children, one that had lived with her husband, of an unblamable conversation, and a grave, sober, ancient woman and of good breeding as to the outward, as men account." She is recorded as having protested in these words: "That it was evident they were going to act the works of darkness or else they would have brought them forth publicly and have declared their offenses that all may hear and fear." Thereupon she was committed to prison and given "ten cruel stripes with a three-fold corded knotted whip." The account goes on to say: "Though ye confessed, when ye had her before you, that for aught ye knew, she had been of an unblamable character, and, though some of you knew her father and called him Mr. Marbery and that she had been well bred (as among men and had so lived) and that she was the mother of many children; yet ye whipped her for all that and moreover told her that ye were likely to have a law to hang her if she came thither again."

Mrs. Scott replied: "If God calls us, woe be to us if we come not and I question not but he whom we love will make us not to count our lives dear unto ourselves for the sake of his name."

Governor John Endicott promptly told her "and we shall be as ready to take away your lives as ye shall be to lay them down."

In June, 1659, her daughter, Patience Scott, age 11 years, accompanied Mary Dyer to Boston to testify in her favor, and was promptly sent to prison. After a delay of three months, she was given a trial, and conducted herself with such discretion and a wisdom far above her years as quite to baffle the magistrates, who could not help admiring her. It would not do to banish such a child, so the court considered that "Satan was put to his shifts to make use of such a child," and ordered her to be sent home.

Regarding her testimony, the account says: "Some of ye confest that ye had many children and that they had been well educated and that it were well if they could say half so much for God as she could for the devil." A short time after, Mrs. Scott's daughter, Mary, went to visit her future husband, Christopher Holden, in prison, and was herself put in prison and kept there a month. Mary Dyer, it will be remembered, was afterwards hung on Boston Common.

In September, 1660, Governor John Winthrop, of Connecticut, received a letter from Roger Williams, in which is the following: "My neighbor, Mrs. Scott, is come from England, and what the whip at Boston could not do, converse with friends in England and their arguments have in a great measure drawn her from the Quakers and wholly from their meetings." She died May 2, 1687, at Newport, R. I., whither she had probably gone upon the death of her husband, to live with her grandson, John Scott.

MARBURY.

DESCENT.	Catherine Marbury married Richard Scott;
whose son,	John Scott, " Rebecca (——);
" "	Silvanus Scott, " Joanna Jenckes;
" daughter,	Esther " " Thomas Sayles;
" son,	John Sayles, " Martha Arnold;
" "	Ishmael Sayles, " Deborah Aldrich;
" "	Arnold " " Lillis Irons;
' daughter,	Deborah " " Raymond Burton;
" "	Adaline Burton, " John W. Thayer.

Mott.

NATHANIEL MOTT came to America probably from Braintree, England, where the Motts were a family noted for their be-
nevolence and interest in church affairs. He first settled at Scituate, Mass., where he is on record as "able to bear arms" as
early as 1643. He soon after removed to Braintree, and,
December 25, 1656, married Anna Shooter, widow of Peter
Shooter. He lived at Braintree during the rest of his life,
which was cut short during the King Philip war. He was
killed by the Indians, February 25, 1675. The raid upon the
town of Braintree that winter day resulted in the death of four
of its citizens, three men and one woman. The woman was not
killed outright, but was carried six or seven miles, and then, in
an unseemly and barbarous manner, was hung up by the roadside between Braintree and Bridgewater. The only one of the
four killed whose name has been ascertained was that of Nathaniel Mott.

ELIZABETH MOTT, daughter of Nathaniel and Anna
(Shooter) Mott, was born at Braintree, Mass, December 5,
1666, and married Edmond Littlefield, Jr., son of Francis and
Rebecca (——) Littlefield, of Wells, Maine, about 1685. She
died (probably) at Braintree.

DESCENT.	Elizabeth Mott	married	Edmond Littlefield, Jr.;
whose daughter,	Elizabeth Littlefield,	"	William Linfield;
" son,	William Linfield,	"	Jemima Clark;
" daughter,	Sarah "	"	Reuben Thayer;
" son,	Caleb Thayer,	"	Patience Phillips;
" son,	John W. "	"	Adaline Burton.

(80)

Mowry.

ROGER MOWRY, by a tradition of the family said to be a cousin or kinsman in some degree of Roger Williams, came from England, and settled at Plymouth, Mass., as early as 1631. In 1636 he had been admitted a member of the church at Salem, of which Roger Williams was pastor. The next year he undertook, "with the help of another sufficient man," to care for the town's cattle. He was to be ready at the pen gate an hour after sunrise each day to take them, and those who did not have their cattle ready were to bring them after the herd. For each head, "all except bulls," he was to have seven shillings, to be paid " always one quarter beforehand." This price, some years later, was reduced to five shillings. Removing from Salem to Providence, R. I., about 1643, he was in 1655 appointed to keep a house of entertainment, and instructed to "set out at the most perspicuous place of said house a convenient sign to give notice to strangers." This occupation may account for his "entering" thirteen ankers of rum and two barrels of sack the next year. In 1657, January 27, he was allowed by the town six pence "for this day's firing and house room." He died, January 5, 1666, at Providence. His wife, Mary Johnson, daughter of John and Margery (——) Johnson, of Roxbury, Mass., was a kinswoman of Isaac Heath, of Roxbury, and they were married previous to 1637, probably while at Salem.

NATHANIEL MOWRY, son of Roger and Mary (Johnson) Mowry, was born at Providence, R. I., in 1644. He married Joanna Inman, daughter of Edward and (——) Inman, of Smithfield, in 1666, at which place he died, March 24, 1718.

MARY MOWRY, daughter of Nathaniel and Joanna (Inman) Mowry, was born at Smithfield, R. I., in 1675, and about

MOWRY.

1694 married John Arnold, son of Richard and Mary (Angell) Arnold, of Providence. In 1731 they removed to Smithfield, where she died, January 27, 1742.

DESCENT.	Mary Mowry	married	John Arnold;
whose son,	William Arnold,	"	Hannah Whipple;
" daughter,	Martha	"	John Sayles;
" son,	Ishmael Sayles,	"	Deborah Aldrich;
" son,	Arnold	"	Lillis Irons;
" daughter,	Deborah	"	Raymond Burton;
" "	Adaline Burton,	"	John W. Thayer.

Mowry.

JOHN MOWRY, son of Roger and Mary (Johnson) Mowry, was born at Providence, R. I., about 1645, and married Mary (——). In 1666 he and Edward Inman bought 2,000 acres of land in the northern part of the state in the present vicinity of Smithfield, "to have and to hold without any trouble or molestation by any Indians." During the King Philip war he "staid and went not away" when invited by the people of Portsmouth to take refuge on the island. For thus facing the danger he afterward shared in the disposition of the captive Indians, whose services were sold for a term of years. He died, July 7, 1690, at Smithfield, and he and his wife were buried on Sayles Hill.

MARY MOWRY, daughter of John and Mary (——) Mowry, was born at Providence, R. I., about 1665, and married James Phillips, son of Michael and Barbara (——) Phillips, of Newport, about 1685. They settled at Providence, and later at Smithfield, where she probably died.

DESCENT.	Mary Mowry	married	James Phillips;
whose son,	Michael Phillips,	"	Freelove Wilkinson;
" "	James "	"	—— ——;
" "	Thomas "	"	Catherine Johnson;
" daughter,	Patience "	"	Caleb Thayer;
" son,	John W. Thayer,	"	Adaline Burton.

(83)

Mowry.

HANNAH MOWRY, daughter of Roger and Mary (Johnson) Mowry, was born at Providence, R. I., September 28, 1656, and married Benjamin Sherman, son of Philip and Sarah (Odding) Sherman, of Portsmouth, December 3, 1674. She died at Portsmouth, before her husband's death, which occurred in 1718.

DESCENT.   Hannah Mowry married Benjamin Sherman;
whose daughter, Deborah Sherman, "   Elisha Johnson;
"   son,   Ebenezer Johnson, "   Elizabeth Tingley;
"   daughter, Catherine   "   "   Thomas Phillips;
"   "   Patience Phillips, "   Caleb Thayer;
"   son,   John W. Thayer, "   Adaline Burton.

Mullins.

WILLIAM MULLINS, one of the unfortunates who came in the Mayflower, left Holland with his wife, two children, Joseph and Priscilla, and a servant, Robert Carter. They had been at Plymouth scarcely two months before he succumbed to the hardships and suffering to which the Pilgrims were exposed, and died, February 21, 1621. His wife, from the same causes, died a few days either before or after her husband, and Joseph and the servant were numbered among the dead before spring. Priscilla alone survived of the family of five. William Mullins was apparently a shoemaker, if his stock in trade was an indication. He contributed, as his share towards the stock of the Mayflower party, twenty-one dozen of shoes and thirteen pairs of boots.

PRISCILLA MULLINS, daughter of William and (———) Mullins, was born probably in England, and came with her father to this country in the party of Pilgrims that sailed in the Mayflower, in 1620. She was left an orphan in a few months by the death of her father and mother, she alone surviving of a family of five. Soon after, she married John Alden, a man afterwards famous in the early history of the colony, and probably died at Duxbury, Mass. "Miles Standish's Courtship" of Priscilla, and other literature relating to her husband, all easily accessible, makes further mention of her here unnecessary.

DESCENT.	Priscilla Mullins	married	John Alden;
whose daughter,	Ruth Alden,	"	John Bass;
" "	Sarah Bass,	"	Ephraim Thayer;
" son,	Joseph Thayer,	"	Eunice Ludden;
" "	Reuben Thayer,	"	Sarah Linfield;
" "	Caleb "	"	Patience Phillips;
" "	John W. "	"	Adaline Burton.

(85)

Olney.

THOMAS OLNEY, one of the Baptists notified to depart from Massachusetts or appear at the next court, was born at St. Albans, Hertford County, England, in 1600, and came to this country in the ship, "Planter," from London, in 1635. Several years before his departure he married Mary Small, of St. Albans, who, besides two sons, came to America with him. He was a shoemaker by trade, and settled at Salem, Mass. In 1638, he and several others were licensed to depart from Mass. Not going immediately they were ordered "to appear at the next court (if they be not gone before) to answer such things as shall be objected." They went. In October of the same year he had settled at Providence, where he was one of the twelve original members of the First Baptist Church, organized in 1639. His former pastor at Salem, in explaining in a letter to a brother pastor the cause of Thomas Olney's expulsion from Salem, wrote: "He wholly refused to hear the church, denying it and all the churches in the Bay to be true churches. The great censure of this, our church, was passed upon him." At Providence he was twice chosen treasurer of the town, was six times appointed commissioner, was nine times chosen assistant, four times deputy, and was for eight years a member of the town council. His homestead was south of the present state house, Arsenal Lane now running through it. In 1643 he bought land and settled at Warwick. In 1656 he was chosen judge to try cases where the amount involved did not exceed forty shillings.

Thomas Olney was a first-class surveyor, and it is said that as he entered upon the surrounding lands with his field book, chain and compass, and mystic words, with the peculiar dignity of official characters of that day, he may well have inspired the Indians with profound awe and led them to feel that no Indian could henceforth dwell upon that part of their tribal property again. He died at Providence in 1682. During the early settlement of New England it was claimed in Connecticut that if a man was too bad to live with in Massachusetts, they sent him to Rhode Island, and when they found one a little too good, they sent him to Connecticut, while the remainder of tolerable and average orthodoxy and respectability were allowed to remain undisturbed.

THOMAS OLNEY, son of Thomas and Mary (Small) Olney, and a prominent Baptist clergyman at Providence, R. I., was born at St. Albans, Hertford County, England, in 1632, and came to this country with his father, in the ship, "Planter," from London, in 1635. From Salem, Mass., in 1638, he came to Providence, where, July 3, 1660, he married Elizabeth Moseley. In 1655, five years before, at the age of twenty-three, he was implicated in a religious tumult, or more strictly, under the pretense of holding a training, he, with others, engaged in an armed resistance to authority. No serious results followed. In 1668, at the age of thirty-six, he was ordained pastor of the First Baptist Church. In a controversy a few years later, with George Fox, the Quaker, the Rev. Thomas Olney is said to have answered Fox in an article, entitled "Ambition Anatomized," with "unseemly severity." He held many public offices. For thirty-seven years he was town clerk; for thirty years, a member of the town council; for fourteen years, a deputy, and for six years, assistant. He was also "proprietor's surveyor." In 1698 he was appointed on a committee "to meet the Connecticut gentlemen to treat before Lord Bellemont about the western bounds of the colony." In 1699 he was chosen "agent for the colony to go to England for maintaining of liberties granted in our charter." This appointment he declined. He died at Providence, June 11, 1722. The inventory of his estate included "fifty-five bound books and twenty-three small unbound books." His wife died about the same time and place. His

OLNEY.

homestead was near the present location of the American Screw Co.'s works, at the foot of Stampers Hill, and he also owned large tracts of land in North Providence and Lincoln.

ELIZABETH OLNEY, daughter of Thomas and Elizabeth (Moseley) Olney, was born at Providence, R. I., January 31, 1666, and married John Sayles, son of John and Mary (Williams) Sayles, of Providence, about 1688. She died in 1699. Her grave and that of her son, Daniel, were still to be found in 1894, west of the railroad track, nearly opposite the foot of Earl street, in Providence. Her grave could be identified among a clump of trees by a head-stone marked simply "E. S., 1699."

DESCENT.		Elizabeth Olney	married	John Sayles;
whose son,		Thomas Sayles,	"	Esther Scott;
"	"	John "	"	Martha Arnold;
"	"	Ishmael "	"	Deborah Aldrich;
"	"	Arnold "	"	Lillis Irons;
"	daughter,	Deborah "	"	Raymond Burton;
"	"	Adaline Burton,	"	John W. Thayer.

Osborne.

JOHN OSBORNE and his wife, Mary, came to this country and had settled at Weymouth, Mass., before 1640, where they raised a family of children. He died at Weymouth, October 27, 1686.

PATIENCE OSBORNE, daughter of John and Mary (——) Osborne, was born at Weymouth, Mass., about 1640-5, and married Joseph Aldrich, son of George and Catherine (——) Aldrich, of Braintree, February 26, 1662. In 1687, they moved to Providence, R. I., where she died in 1705, or soon after.

DESCENT.	Patience Osborne	married	Joseph Aldrich;
whose son,	Samuel Aldrich,	"	Jane (——);
" "	" "	"	Hannah (——);
" "	" "	"	Elizabeth Keeler;
" daughter,	Deborah "	"	Ishmael Sayles;
" son,	Arnold Sayles,	"	Lillis Irons;
" daughter,	Deborah "	"	Raymond Burton;
" "	Adaline Burton,	"	John W. Thayer.

Parkhurst.

GEORGE PARKHURST, one of the early settlers of Water-town, Mass., came to this country about 1635, with two children. It is not certain that his wife came with him, but, if so, she died soon after settling at Watertown. In November, 1643, he married Susanna Simpson, widow of John Simpson, of Watertown, and in a short time removed to Boston, where he died.

PHŒBE PARKHURST, daughter of George and (——) Park-hurst, was born in England, and, about 1635, came to this country with her parents. About 1640, she married, as his second wife, Thomas Arnold, of Watertown, Mass. In 1661, they moved to Providence, R. I., where she died in 1688, or soon after.

DESCENT.		Phœbe Parkhurst	married	Thomas Arnold;
whose son,		Richard Arnold,	"	Mary Angell;
"	"	John	"	Mary Mowry;
"	"	William	"	Hannah Whipple;
"	daughter,	Martha	"	John Sayles;
"	son,	Ishmael Sayles,	"	Deborah Aldrich,
"	"	Arnold	"	Lillis Irons;
"	daughter,	Deborah	"	Raymond Burton;
"	"	Adaline Burton,	"	John W. Thayer.

(90)

Pemberton.

ROBERT PEMBERTON, maternal grandfather of Roger Williams, and his wife, Catherine (——), were residents of St. Albans, Hertfordshire, England, where they died the latter part of the 16th century.

ALICE PEMBERTON, mother of Roger Williams and daughter of Robert and Catherine (——) Pemberton, was born at St. Albans, Hertfordshire, England, in 1564. About 1590, she married James Williams, of St. Albans, and not long after they moved to London, where she died in January, 1634. In her will she left £10 yearly, for twenty years, to her son, Roger, "now beyond the seas;" or, in case of his death, to his wife and daughter. She provided for the distribution of bread to the poor on the day of her funeral and left money for a supper for her tenants

DESCENT.	Alice Pemberton	married	James Williams;
whose son,	Roger Williams,	"	Mary (——);
" daughter,	Mary "	"	John Sayles;
" son,	John Sayles,	"	Elizabeth Olney;
" "	Thomas "	"	Esther Scott;
" "	John "	"	Martha Arnold;
" "	Ishmael "	"	Deborah Aldrich;
" "	Arnold "	"	Lillis Irons;
" daughter.	Deborah "	"	Raymond Burton;
" "	Adaline Burton,	"	John W. Thayer.

(91)

Phillips.

MICHAEL PHILLIPS, of Newport, R. I., was admitted a freeman in that place in 1668. He died about 1689, and his wife, Barbara, married Edward Inman, of Providence, soon after, and removed to that town. She died about 1706.

JAMES PHILLIPS, son of Michael and Barbara (——) Phillips, was born at Newport, R. I., about 1665, and married Mary Mowry, daughter of John and Mary (——) Mowry, of Providence. He settled first at Providence, and, in 1733, at Smithfield, where he died, December 12, 1746.

MICHAEL PHILLIPS, son of James and Mary (Mowry) Phillips, was born at Providence, R. I., about 1690, and married Freelove Wilkinson, daughter of John and Deborah (Whipple) Wilkinson, of Providence. They settled at Smithfield, where he probably died.

JAMES PHILLIPS, son of Michael and Freelove (Wilkinson) Phillips, was born, probably, at Providence, R. I., about 1725, and, after living for a time at Smithfield, removed to Coventry, where he probably died. Nothing is known of his wife.

THOMAS PHILLIPS, son of James Phillips, was born at Coventry, R. I., in 1762, and at the age of 16 entered the Revolutionary army, taking part in the battle of Rhode Island. In 1788, he married Catherine Johnson, daughter of Ebenezer and Elizabeth (Tingley) Johnson, of Coventry, R. I. They settled at Sterling, Conn., on the "Kettle farm." He is remembered as a man who never used profane or vulgar language. He died at Sterling, January 31, 1833.

PHILLIPS.

PATIENCE PHILLIPS, daughter of Thomas and Catherine (Johnson) Phillips, was born at Sterling, Conn., in 1792, and married, as his second wife, Caleb Thayer, of Sterling, son of Reuben and Sarah (Linfield) Thayer, of Randolph, Mass. She had done housework for him after the death of his first wife and before his second marriage. In appearance, she was tall and had a bright, lively, cheerful disposition. She died, April 15, 1834, and was buried in Cedar Swamp burying ground on the road from Ekonk to Oneco.

DESCENT. Patience Phillips married Caleb Thayer;
whose son, John W. Thayer, '' Adaline Burton.

Potter.

ROBERT POTTER, the death of whose wife was afterwards
caused by the exposure and hardships suffered at Warwick,
R. I., when that place was besieged by the Massachusetts
troops, came to this country from Coventry, England, in 1630,
and first settled on Boston street at Lynn, Mass. He was a
farmer by occupation and was soon admitted freeman. In
1634 he had removed to Roxbury. His presence in Massachusetts was not, however, to be tolerated for any length of
time, and, in May, 1638, he was warned by the General Court
to remove out of the colony. He went that year. He was
admitted as an inhabitant of the island of Aquidneck, R. I.,
that fall, and the next spring, with twenty-eight others, signed
the civil compact. In 1640, however, friction arose, and the
General Court passed a vote that "if he come upon the island
armed he shall, by the constable (calling to him sufficient aid)
be disarmed and carried before the magistrate and there find
surety for his good behavior." In 1642, he sold his house and
land at Portsmouth, and settled, with Samuel Gorton and
several others, at Warwick. In 1643, in September, he and
others were summoned to Boston to answer some complaints
made by Indian chiefs. The Warwick men claimed they were
outside the jurisdiction of Massachusetts, and refused to
answer the summons. Soldiers from Boston were accordingly
sent and besieged the inhabitants of Warwick in a fortified
house. The charge of holding "blasphemous errors," of
which they must repent, was then made against them. The
house was finally captured and the men taken to Boston for
trial. The women and children were driven into the woods
and their homes burned behind them. The hardships suffered
resulted in the death of three of the women at least, one of
whom was the wife of Robert Potter. He was brought before

POTTER.

court in November, charged with heresy and sedition, and was sentenced to prison during the pleasure of the court. In addition he was charged not to speak against the church or state, or preach his heresies or break jail, or, on conviction, he should die. He was sent to Rowley and kept in confinement, "wearing such bolts or irons as may hinder his escape," till the next March, when he was banished, both from Massachusetts and Warwick. He returned to Warwick, however, and was not again disturbed. In 1649, he was licensed to keep an inn, and in 1651 was appointed commissioner. In 1655, he was again appointed to keep a house of entertainment, and a convenient sign was to be set out at the most perspicuous place to give notice to strangers. He died that year. Bishop Alonzo Potter, of Pennsylvania, Bishop Horatio Potter, Bishop Henry C. Potter and Hon. Clarkson N. Potter, all of New York, are lineal descendants of Robert Potter.

—— POTTER, daughter of Robert and —— Potter, was born in England, and came to this country with her father in 1630. When Warwick was sacked by the Massachusetts troops in 1643, she was driven into the woods with many others, and her home was reduced to ashes. She married Henry Knowles, of Warwick, and died in 1670, or after.

DESCENT.		—— Potter	married	Henry Knowles;
whose daughter,		Mary Knowles,	"	Moses Lippitt;
"	"	Martha Lippitt,	"	Thomas Burlingame;
"	"	Persis Burlingame,	"	William Burton;
"	son,	Benjamin Burton,	"	Alice Westcott;
"	"	Edmond	"	Lucretia Boardman;
"	"	Raymond	"	Deborah Sayles;
"	daughter,	Adaline	"	John W. Thayer.

Priest.

JAMES PRIEST and his wife, Lydia, came to this country and settled at Weymouth, Mass., as early as 1640. They probably lived and died there. He died in 1676.

DELIVERANCE PRIEST, daughter of James and Lydia (——) Priest, was born at Weymouth, Mass., in 1644, and married Shadrach Thayer, son of Thomas and Margery (Wheeler) Thayer, of Braintree, July 12, 1661. She died at Braintree, January 17, 1723, and her grave, in 1894, could be seen in the old cemetery, a short distance west of the railroad station, at North Braintree.

DESCENT.			
whose son,	Deliverance Priest married		Shadrach Thayer;
" "	Ephraim Thayer,	"	Sarah Bass;
" "	Joseph "	"	Eunice Ludden;
" "	Reuben "	"	Sarah Linfield;
" "	Caleb "	"	Patience Phillips;
' "	John W. "	"	Adaline Burton.

Sayles.

JOHN SAYLES, the progenitor of a noteworthy Rhode Island family, was born in Manchester, England, in 15—, and came to this country in 1635, in his own vessel, with his wife, two sons and several daughters. They first settled at Portsmouth, R. I.

JOHN SAYLES, son of John Sayles, of Manchester, England, was brought to this country, by his father, in 1635, at the age of two years, and, after living for a time at Portsmouth, R. I., he came to Providence, where, about 1650, he married Mary Williams, daughter of Roger and Mary (——) Williams, of Providence. In 1653 he was treasurer of the Assembly which met at Providence, May 16. In 1656 he "entered an anker of liquor." The same year he assisted Thomas Angell in rescuing a prisoner from the custody of a Massachusetts officer. In 1657 he was empowered "to treat with the Indians that lay claim to the meadows of Lohusqussuck, and clear it for the town and the above mentioned be accommodated therein." In 1677 he was fined twenty shillings for not attending grand jury. During the thirty years or thereabouts, from the time of his marriage till his death, he was at different times commissioner, town clerk, town treasurer, warden, grand juror, a member of the town council, and he was twelve times chosen assistant or deputy. He died in 1681, and his grave with that of his wife and son-in-law, William Greene, can be found in the Easton burial ground, near Sachuset Beach, Middletown, R. I.

JOHN SAYLES, son of John and Mary (Williams) Sayles, was born at Providence, R. I, August 17, 1654, and married Elizabeth Olney, daughter of Thomas and Elizabeth (Moseley) Olney, of Providence, about 1688. He owned a large stock-

(97)

farm containing 250 acres, near Mashapauge, in Providence, which he sold in 1703, "reserving forever two poles square where several graves are contained about thirty rods west of the house." This reference is doubtless to the graves of his wife and son, Daniel, both of whom were then dead, and whose graves in 1894 could be found west of the railroad track nearly opposite the foot of Earl street, among a small clump of trees. His wife's grave can be identified by a head-stone marked simply " E. S., 1699." John Sayles afterwards opened a hotel, his license "to keep a publick house and sell liquor" being dated August 14, 1710. In 1694 and again in 1706, he was appointed deputy. He died at Providence, August 2, 1727.

THOMAS SAYLES, son of John and Elizabeth (Olney) Sayles, was born at Providence, R. I., February 9, 1699, and married Esther Scott, daughter of Silvanus and Joanna (Jenckes) Scott, of Smithfield, December 14, 1721. He settled at Smithfield, in 1731, where he accumulated quite an estate. He acted as moderator of the town for six years, was town clerk nine years, was two years a member of the town council, and was three times chosen deputy. He died, November 9, 1754, leaving an estate valued at £3,654. His farm was, in 1894, known as the Durrans farm, and was situated about a mile directly east of Primrose railroad station, and on the western slope of Sayles Hill. The homestead was south of the road running east over Sayles Hill, midway between that road and the " white " school-house. About a quarter of a mile back of the house, up in the lots to the east, the writer found the graves of both Thomas Sayles and his wife, Esther. The burial lot was enclosed by a substantial stone-wall, and near the entrance was a huge boulder. The inscriptions were still clearly discernible.

COLONEL JOHN SAYLES, one of the prominent men of Rhode Island during the war of the Revolution, was the son of

SAYLES.

Thomas and Esther (Scott) Sayles, and was born at Smithfield, R. I., January 6, 1723. He married Martha Arnold, daughter of William and Hannah (Whipple) Arnold, of Smithfield, December 19, 1742. During the Revolutionary war, and several times before and after, he was chosen assistant, and early took an active part in the military affairs of the state, serving as captain as far back as 1754. In 1775 he was appointed on a committee to prepare an act for the purpose of raising a regiment of soldiers for the defense of the colony. In 1776 he was chosen colonel of the regiment. In 1778 the legislature passed a resolution ordering a bill of £36 paid him "for small arms etc. for the use of the militia of Smithfield during the late expedition against Rhode Island." In 1780 he was appointed to receive recruits in the town of Smithfield. In 1788, June 24, when the news was received of the adoption of the Federal constitution by the requisite number of states, an invitation was sent from Providence to several of the surrounding towns, including Smithfield, to join with Providence in an appropriate celebration of the event. The country towns opposed to the Federal constitution were alike opposed to celebrating its adoption, and the night before the date fixed by Providence for the celebration, July 4, the citizens of Smithfield and the surrounding towns met on the plains north of the Cove, in numbers estimated at nearly 1,000 men, many of them coming armed. An ox was being roasted, and other preparations for the event the next day were being made. Blood-shed seemed imminent. A committee of reconciliation between the town and country was soon appointed, however, and it was finally agreed no reference to the adoption of the constitution should be made next day, either in the speeches or toast. Thus the trouble was amicably settled. Colonel John Sayles was a member of the committee of reconciliation from the country. In 1790 he was a delegate to the Rhode Island Constitutional Convention, and, March 3, made a motion to appoint a committee to draft a bill of rights and amendments to be proposed to

(99)

SAYLES.

the Federal constitution. On a loose piece of paper returned with the minutes of the convention was the motion, in writing, signed by John Sayles. He was appointed on the committee. When the bill adopting the Federal constitution came up for action, he voted against it. Colonel Sayles was said to have been a very pious man. The date of his death has not yet been discovered.

ISHMAEL SAYLES, son of Colonel John and Martha (Arnold) Sayles, was born at Smithfield, R. I., December 1, 1751, and married Deborah Aldrich, daughter of "Swearing Sam" and Elizabeth (Keeler) Aldrich, of Smithfield, October 7, 1773. During the war of the American Revolution he joined the state militia and took part in the battle of Rhode Island, in August, 1778. He had, at the time, settled on a farm bought for him by his father, on Buck Hill, in the town of Burrillville, and when the call came for volunteers he left his wife, with three children, to care for the farm, and went to the defense of the colony. He died, November 5 or 9, 1793, and was buried on his farm. His grave, with that of his wife, was, in 1894, near the main road from Pascoag to East Thompson, Conn., two and one-half miles west of Pascoag, on what was then known as the "Staples" farm. The graves were a short distance off in the lots to the north of a lane leading west from a cross-road that ran south one-quarter of a mile from the main road above mentioned. It is said the subject of this sketch desired to be buried on his own land, so that upon the morning of Resurrection day he could be close by and on hand early to claim his farm against all comers.

ARNOLD SAYLES, son of Ishmael and Deborah (Aldrich) Sayles, was born, probably, at Smithfield, R. I., December 1, 1773, before his father's removal to the farm in the town of Burrillville. He married Lillis Irons, daughter of Captain Jeremiah and Barbery (Tucker) Irons, of Burrillville, February 27, 1795. His farm, half a mile south of Tarkiln saw mill, was

(100)

where he raised his family of children, thirteen in all. He was in appearance, tall and spare, with blue eyes, and his children remembered him as a father who never whipped them or interfered with their childish plans. His daughter, Lillis, one Sunday morning took the cat into bed with her, and her father told her to give it up to her sister in another bed. This Lillis stoutly refused to do, and the result was, the cat remained, and showed its appreciation of its present comfortable quarters by purring more loudly than ever. This little incident was told the writer by Lillis (Eddy) in the summer of 1892. Arnold Sayles was a first-class carpenter and machinist, and worked at his trade till he was far advanced in life. He lived for several years at Chepachet, down on the "Point," where he died, May 6, 1860. His grave, with that of his wife, in 1894, was in the back part of the old cemetery on the "Plains" between Chepachet and Mapleville.

DEBORAH SAYLES, daughter of Arnold and Lillis (Irons) Sayles, was born at Cooperstown, N. Y., March 18, 1798, where her parents lived for a short time. They soon returned to Chepachet, R. I., where, May 6, 1814, she married Raymond Burton, son of Edmond and Lucretia (Boardman) Burton, of Cranston. They settled at Chepachet, afterward living for a time at Burrillville and Waterford. During her girlhood she was trained to do the work of a family of thirteen, and grew up a strong, healthy woman. She was an excellent housekeeper, neat and orderly, and was the main stay of the family for years. She was also prudent, self-denying and high-minded, teaching her children to prize education and intelligence and despise meanness and vulgarity. She accumulated property sufficient to support herself in her old age, notwithstanding the misfortune attending her husband's insanity, and died at Pascoag, July 6, 1881. She was buried beside her husband, on Acote's Hill, Chepachet.

DESCENT.　　Deborah Sayles married Raymond Burton;
whose daughter, Adaline Burton,　　"　　John W. Thayer.

(101)

Scott.

EDWARD SCOTT, grandfather of the first one of the family name to emigrate to this country, was born at Glemsford, Suffolk County, England, about the middle of the 16th century. His wife was Elizabeth Grome. The name, Scott, has been traced, in Satchel's history, back to the 8th century, but it was unknown in England until the reign of Edward I. Edward Scott was a descendant of the Scotts of Scotts-Hall, from the close of the 15th century, and his son, Richard, probably derived his given name from Sir Richard Woodville, whose family was connected with the Scotts by marriage about 1450.

RICHARD SCOTT, son of Edward and Elizabeth (Grome) Scott, was born at Glemsford, Suffolk County, England, the last of the 16th century. His wife was Margaret Haney.

RICHARD SCOTT, son of Richard and Margaret (Haney) Scott, and the only one of the family name who is recorded as having emigrated to New England during the first half of the 17th century, was born at Glemsford, Suffolk County, England, in 1607, and came to this country in the ship, "Griffin," in 1634. Benjamin Scott, chamberlain of London, in his address upon the occasion of the laying of the corner stone of the Pilgrim Church, of Southwark, in 1864, said: "Some of my family (the Scotts of Scotts-Hall) went over in the ship 'Griffin' with the Rev. John Lothrup." Richard Scott joined the church at Boston, August 28, 1634. He was a shoemaker by trade, and first settled at Ipswich, Mass. His wife, Catherine Marbury, daughter of the Rev. Francis and Bridget (Dryden) Marbury, of London, he probably married before coming to this country. Governor Winthrop, of Massachusetts, in his journal of November 24, 1634, relates this incident: "One

(102)

SCOTT.

Scott and Eliot, of Ipswich, were lost in their way homewards, and wandered up and down six days and eat nothing. At length they were found by an Indian, being almost senseless for want of rest." In 1637, finding his presence was not longer desired in Massachusetts, he removed to Providence, R. I., and, with twelve others, signed a civil compact for a form of town government. In 1640 he and thirty-eight others signed a compact providing for arbitration. It is said he was the first resident Quaker at Providence. The suffering inflicted by the Boston authorities during the Quaker persecutions upon his wife and children is referred to elsewhere. In 1678, in a letter to George Fox, he wrote as follows:

"Friends: Concerning the conversation and carriage of this man, Roger Williams, I have been his neighbor these thirty-eight years. I have only been absent in the time of the wars with the Indians till this present. I walked with him in the Baptists' way about three or four months, but in that short time of his standing I discovered he must have the ordering of all their affairs, or else there would be no quiet agreement amongst them. * * * That which took most with him and was his life, was to get honor amongst men, especially amongst the great ones." The letter refers to Roger Williams' return with the charter and his being met at Seakonk by his neighbors in fourteen canoes. "And the man being hemmed in in the middle of the canoes, was so elevated and transported out of himself that I was condemned in myself that amongst the rest I had been an instrument to set him up in his pride and folly. And he that before could reprove my wife for asking her two sons why they did not pull off their hats to him, and told her she might as well bid them pull off their shoes as their hats (though afterwards she took him in the same act and turned his reproof upon his own head). And he that could not put off his cap at prayer in his worship can now put it off to every man or boy that pulls off his hat to him." Mr. Scott also charged him with inconsistency in professing

SCOTT.

liberty of conscience and yet persecuting those who did not join in his views.

At one time Richard Scott was the heaviest taxpayer but one in Rhode Island. He took an active part in the early Indian wars. He died in 1680. A portion of the original Scott estate in Smithfield had, until 1825, always been owned by a lineal descendant of Richard Scott. That year it passed out of the family upon being sold to the Lonsdale Company. A few years after his death a deposition regarding the distribution of a portion of his property was recorded as follows: "Nine years since, or thereabout, being on board of the vessel that then Henry Beere was master of, there being also aboard Richard Scott, he desired deponents to come to him into the cabin, and declared that he desired," etc. Possibly this was a case of sea-sickness.

JOHN SCOTT, a victim of Indian treachery, near Pawtucket Ferry, R. I., was born probably at Ipswich, Mass., about 1635. He was the son of Richard and Catherine (Marbury) Scott, who came from England in 1634, and stopped for a short time at Ipswich. In 1637 they came to Providence, R. I., where John, about 1660, married Rebecca (———), and settled near Pawtucket Ferry. From time to time he added to his landed estate. Once, in 1668, he complained of a neighbor for "entering" upon a portion of his land. He was chosen deputy in 1666. In 1671, at his request, the town voted "to lay out a highway to Mr. Blackstone's river, where it may be most convenient." The tradition seems to be well established that John Scott met his death by being shot by an Indian in the doorway of his own house. Roger Williams, in a letter to John Winthrop, Jr., dated June 27, 1675, referred to his death as follows: "Some say John Scot at Pawtucket Ferry is slain." The effect of the shot seems not to have proved immediately fatal, for it is thought he afterwards made his will. At a court martial held at Newport, August 25, 1676, an Indian, charged with the

SCOTT.

crime, proved an alibi and that he "was not at the wounding of John Scot." His wife, Rebecca, is recorded as a widow November 8, 1677, and died about 1701.

SILVANUS SCOTT, son of John and Rebecca (———) Scott, was born at Pawtucket Falls, R. I., November 10, 1672, and in 1692 married Joanna Jenckes, daughter of Joseph and Esther (Ballard) Jenckes, of Providence. Not long after he settled at Smithfield. He was twice appointed deputy, in 1709 and again in 1717, and was a member of the town council for six years. In 1716 he was granted liberty, with two others, "to use and improve so much of Starve Goat Island as shall be needful for their making, drying and securing of fish on said island during their following the trade of fishing." He died January 13, 1742, leaving an estate valued at £3,664. Among the items inventoried was a "negro man," valued at £60. Two years later, upon the death of his wife, the same negro man is inventoried as "worth nothing."

ESTHER SCOTT, daughter of Sylvanus and Joanna (Jenckes) Scott, was born at Smithfield, R. I., December 5, 1700, and married Thomas Sayles, son of John and Elizabeth (Olney) Sayles, of Providence, December 14, 1721. She died at Smithfield, in 1786, outliving her husband thirty-four years. The inscription over her grave (see Thomas Sayles) gave the date of her death, "July 7, 1786."

DESCENT.	Esther Scott	married	Thomas Sayles;
whose son,	John Sayles,	''	Martha Arnold;
'' ''	Ishmael ''	''	Deborah Aldrich;
'' ''	Arnold ''	''	Lillis Irons;
'' daughter,	Deborah ''	''	Raymond Burton;
' ''	Adaline Burton,	''	John W. Thayer.

Sherman.

THOMAS SHERMAN, the earliest known paternal ancestor of General W. T. Sherman and Senator John Sherman, was of Dedham, Essex County, England. The name was derived from the early occupation of the family: to wit, cloth dressers, or shearers of cloth. The family at Dedham retained the trade and also the coat of arms worn by that branch of the family residing in or about London. Thomas Sherman came to Dedham probably from the county of Suffolk, and was buried at Dedham, March 16, 1554.

HENRY SHERMAN, son of Thomas Sherman, was born in the county of Suffolk, England, and came with his father to Dedham, where he died in 1589. His wife was Agnes Butler, and she died in 1580.

HENRY SHERMAN, son of Henry and Agnes (Butler) Sherman, was born at Dedham, Essex County, England, and about 1570 married Susan Hills. He was a clothier by trade, and died in August, 1610. His wife died in September of the same year.

SAMUEL SHERMAN, son of Henry and Susan (Hills) Sherman, was born at Dedham, Essex County, England, in 1573. He married Phillippa Ward, and died at Dedham, in 1615 His wife survived him a few years.

PHILIP SHERMAN, son of Samuel and Phillippa (Ward) Sherman, was born at Dedham, Essex County, England, February 5, 1610. He came to this country in 1633, a single man, settling in a short time at Roxbury, Mass. He was admitted a freeman the next year. In 1637 he took the popular side in the

(106)

SHERMAN.

Ann Hutchinson troubles, but soon was "disarmed," or, in other words, warned to deliver up all guns, pistols, swords, powder, shot, etc. This was because "the opinions and revelations of Mr. Wheelwright and Mrs. Hutchinson had seduced and led into dangerous errors many of the people here in New England." This occurred in November. In March, 1638, the General Court issued an order for him to appear at court, "to answer to such things as shall be objected, if he be not gone before." But he had gone before. He left, intending to settle in New Hampshire, but the climate was so severe he abandoned his land and removed to Rhode Island. He is recorded as having signed, with eighteen others, a compact at Portsmouth, R. I., five days before the order for his arrest was issued. In 1640 he was chosen, with four others, to lay out lands. In 1665, and again in 1667, he was chosen deputy. When the regular government was established at Portsmouth, in 1639, he was chosen the first secretary, and continued to hold the position for four years. Those early records, prepared by him, still remain at Portsmouth, and show him to have been a neat and even expert penman, as well as an educated man. He was a Quaker, and is said to have been a very devout but a determined man. He was a person of intelligence, wealth and influence, and, at critical periods, was frequently consulted by those in authority.

Rev. John Eliot, the apostle to the Indians and the first pastor of the church at Roxbury, says of him:

" Philip Sherman came into this land in 1633, a single man, and after married Sarah Odding, daughter of Margaret, the wife of John Porter, by a former husband. This man was of a melancholy temper. He lived honestly and comfortably among us several years. Upon a just calling went for England and returned again with a blessing. But after his-in-law, John Porter, was so carried away with the opinions and familism and scism, he followed them and removed to the (Rhode) Island.

SHERMAN.

He behaved himself sinfully in those matters (as may appear in the story), and was cast out of the church."

During the King Philip war it was voted "that in these troublesome times and straits in this colony this (Portsmouth) assembly, desiring to have the advice and concurrence of the most judicious inhabitants, if it may be had for the good of the whole, do desire at their next sitting the company and counsel" of sixteen persons. Philip Sherman was among the number. He died at Portsmouth, in 1687, leaving an extensive estate in lands situated in Portsmouth, Narragansett, Ponegansett, Westerly, and Dartmouth, Mass. His wife, Sarah Odding, died in 1681.

BENJAMIN SHERMAN, son of Philip and Sarah (Odding) Sherman, was born at Portsmouth, R. I., in 1650, and, December 3, 1674, married Hannah Mowry, daughter of Roger and Mary (Johnson) Mowry, of Providence. In 1688 he was appointed constable, and in 1707 deputy. He was a farmer, and owned land both in Portsmouth and Kingston. He died, September 19, 1719, at Portsmouth.

DEBORAH SHERMAN, daughter of Benjamin and Hannah (Mowry) Sherman, was born at Portsmouth, R I., September 3, 1691, and married Elisha Johnson, son of John and Elizabeth (——) Johnson, of Westerly. They removed to Coventry, where she died before 1750.

DESCENT.	Deborah Sherman	married	Elisha Johnson;
whose son,	Ebenezer Johnson,	"	Elizabeth Tingley;
" daughter,	Catherine "	"	Thomas Phillips;
" "	Patience Phillips,	"	Caleb Thayer;
" son,	John W. Thayer,	"	Adaline Burton.

(108)

Smith.

CHRISTOPHER SMITH came to Providence, R. I., it is believed, from Lanchester, England, at the same time that his
son-in-law, Lieutenant Lawrence Wilkinson, did, about 1647.
He was on the tax-list at Providence in 1650, was made a freeman in 1655, and served as juryman the same year. He took
the oath of allegiance in 1667. During the King Philip war
he and his wife, Alice, of whom little else is known, went to
Newport when so many took refuge there from the dangers of
an Indian warfare. He died at Newport in June, 1676, "an
ancient Friend of Providence," according to the records. His
wife, Alice, died in 1681, or soon after.

SUSANNA SMITH, daughter of Christopher and Alice
(——) Smith, was born, probably, at Lanchester, England,
where she married Lawrence Wilkinson, son of William and
Mary (Conyers) Wilkinson, of Lanchester. They came to this
country in 1645–47, and settled at Providence, R. I., where she
died previous to 1692.

DESCENT.	Susanna Smith	married	Lawrence Wilkinson;
whose son,	John Wilkinson,	''	Deborah Whipple;
'' daughter,	Freeborn ''	''	Michael Phillips;
'' son,	James Phillips.	''	(—— ——);
'' ''	Thomas ''	''	Catherine Johnson;
'' daughter,	Patience ''	''	Caleb Thayer;
'' son,	John W. Thayer,	''	Adaline Burton.

Staples.

JOHN STAPLES came from the south of England and settled in North Weymouth, Mass., about 1630–5. He lived at the foot of King Oak Hill, in that part of the town known as "Old Spain." He died in August, 1683. In his will he divided his property equally, excepting an acre of salt marsh to his son, John, between his sons and daughters alike.

JOHN STAPLES, son of John Staples, was born at Weymouth, Mass., about 1650–5, and married Jemima Jewett, about 1680. They lived and probably both died at Braintree.

JEMIMA STAPLES, daughter of John and Jemima (Jewett) Staples, was born at Braintree, Mass., April 23, 1694, and married Jonathan Clark, son of Joseph and Damaris (Francis) Clark, October 5, 1711. She died, probably, at Braintree.

DESCENT.	Jemima Staples married Jonathan Clark;
whose daughter, " Clark, "	William Linfield;
" " Sarah Linfield, "	Reuben Thayer;
" son, Caleb Thayer. "	Patience Phillips;
" " John W. Thayer. "	Adaline Burton.

Stream.

ELIZABETH STREAM, a widow with several children, came from England in the early part of the settlement of the Massachusetts colony, and located at Weymouth. For her second husband she married John Otis, whose first wife died in 1653. She died at Weymouth in July, 1676, providing in her will for the payment of a debt of £80 due her son, John Stream, from her son-in-law, John Holbrook.

ELIZABETH STREAM, daughter of Elizabeth Stream by her first husband, was born in England in 1624, and came to this country with her widowed mother a few years later. Soon after 1644 she married Captain John Holbrook, then a widower, of Weymouth, Mass., and died June 25th, 1688.

DESCENT.	Elizabeth Stream married	John Holbrook;
whose daughter,	Eunice Holbrook,	"	Benjamin Ludden;
" son,	Benjamin Ludden,	"	Sarah (——);
" daughter,	Eunice	"	"	Joseph Thayer;
" son,	Reuben Thayer,	"	Sarah Linfield;
" "	Caleb	"	"	Patience Phillips;
" "	John W.	"	"	Adaline Burton.

Tefft.

JOHN TEFFT and his wife, Mary (——), were settled at Portsmouth, R. I., as early as 1653, coming, possibly, from Boston to Rhode Island. In 1671 he had removed tò Kings Town His death, during the King Philip war, is somewhat indefinitely referred to in a letter written by Captain James Oliver, in January, 1676. The marriage of his son, John Tefft, to a Wamponag is first mentioned, and it is said the son shot twenty times at the English in the Narragansett fight. He was afterwards captured and executed at Providence, "a sad wretch, he never heard a sermon but once these fourteen years. His father, going to recall him, lost his head and lies unburied."

TABITHA TEFFT, daughter of John and Mary (——) Tefft, was born at Portsmouth, R. I., in 1653, and married George Gardiner, son of George and Herodias (Long) Gardiner, of Newport. She died at Kings Town, in 1722, or soon after.

DESCENT.	Tabitha Tefft	married	George Gardiner;
whose daughter,	Abigail Gardiner,	"	William Westcott;
" son,	William Westcott,	"	Katherine (——);
" daughter,	Alice	"	Benjamin Burton;
" son,	Edmond Burton,	"	Lucretia Boardman;
" "	Raymond	"	Deborah Sayles;
" daughter,	Adaline	"	John W. Thayer.

Thayer.

THOMAS THAYER, possibly one of two brothers to settle at
Braintree, Mass., about the same time, was a native of Thornbury, Gloucester County, England. He was a shoemaker by
trade, and married Margery Wheeler, April 13, 1618. They
came to this country about 1630, and settled on a large farm in
Braintree. It is an interesting fact that this farm, or portions
of it, have, until recently, continuously remained in the possession of Thomas Thayer or a lineal descendant of his, named
Thayer. In 1892 the last piece of the original farm was sold
by the heirs of Jechonias Thayer, and so the old homestead has
finally passed out of the family possession after 262 years of
continuous ownership. The old homestead was situated about
a quarter of a mile east of the present (North) Braintree railroad station, and the site is now (1894) occupied by a substantial farm-house on the north side of the highway. An iron
mine situated on the farm was successfully worked for several
years, and specimens of iron slag are still to be found there.
Thomas Thayer died June 2, 1665, and was probably buried in
Quincy, then a part of Braintree. He brought with him, from
England, three sons, Thomas, Ferdinando and Shadrach, and
he appears to have had no other children, as no mention is
made of any others in his will. He, however, did state explic-
itly in that document that if any of his children " shall appear
to be discontented and murmur " at the disposition he made of
his property, then he should be cut off with but five shillings,
and his portion divided among the others. His wife died February 11, 1672-3.

SHADRACH THAYER, youngest son of Thomas and Margery (Wheeler) Thayer, was baptized at Thornbury, Gloucester
County, England, May 10, 1629, and was brought to this

(113)

country by his parents about 1630. He married, for his second wife, Deliverance Priest, daughter of James and Lydia Priest, of Weymouth, Mass., July 12, 1661, and upon the death of his father, four years later, continued to live upon the farm, occupying a house some thirty rods from the old homestead in Braintree. He died October 19, 1678, and was probably buried at Braintree.

EPHRAIM THAYER, son of Shadrach and Deliverance (Priest) Thayer, was born at Braintree, Mass., January 17, 1669, and in 1692, January 7, married Sarah Bass, of Roxbury, daughter of John and Ruth (Alden) Bass and granddaughter of John Alden. "This couple were blessed with a numerous family of children remarkable for their piety. On one communion occasion they enjoyed the singular felicity of presenting themselves with the fourteen children God had so graciously given them at the table of our Lord to receive the emblems of His redeeming love. A similar instance has seldom been found in the annals of the Christian church."—*Alden's Collection.*

In 1706 Ephraim Thayer gave the land and was active in the building of a new church, situated just west of the present railroad station at (North) Braintree. He wanted the church called "Naphtali," the name of his tenth child, born about that time. He was one of the prominent men of Braintree, and always lived on the old Thayer homestead. One morning, June 15, 1757, he was found dead near the barn door. It has always been supposed his death was caused by his receiving a violent blow in the forehead from the cross-bar, as he was either going in or out of the barn door. He died at the age of 88 years, and his funeral was attended by a "great concourse of people."—(Church records). His grave can now (1894) be found near the east side of the old burying ground west of the railroad station at (North) Braintree.

JOSEPH THAYER, son of Ephraim and Sarah (Bass) Thayer,

THAYER.

was born at Braintree, Mass., July 28, 1699, and married Eunice Ludden, daughter of Benjamin and Sarah (——) Ludden, of Weymouth, November 16, 1738. He lived on the old Thayer homestead till 1752, when he moved to Randolph, where, the same year, he joined the South Precinct Church by letter. In 1742 Joseph Thayer received from the town six shillings and fourpence for "birds' heads," and again in 1748 a town order was drawn in his favor for nineteen shillings and sixpence for "splitting rocks, powder and mending drills." In 1756 he paid one shilling and fourpence for one-half bushel corn for "one town's poor," but the next year he received from the town three pounds, eleven shillings and seven pence for boarding the "widow Niles." He died at Randolph, January 8, 1778, where he was probably buried.

REUBEN THAYER, son of Joseph and Eunice (Ludden) Thayer, was born at Braintree, Mass., January 27, 1741, and at the age of eleven moved with his father to Randolph, where, in 1767, he joined the church. He married Sarah Linfield, of Braintree, daughter of William and Jemima (Clark) Linfield, September 17, 1768, and late in life moved with her to Sterling, Conn., where he lived with his son, Caleb, till his death, October 24, 1826. Reuben Thayer was a rigid Presbyterian, and during the last years of his life took upon himself the duty of invariably asking a blessing at his son's table. He always insisted upon occupying a certain place by the open fire, and was greatly disturbed whenever a visitor happened to get his accustomed corner by the chimney. In 1816 he was inadvertently crowded out by the writer's great-aunt, Matilda, who was there on a visit to her sister, Patience, his son's second wife. This little incident was related to the writer in 1892 by Matilda, who was then in her 82d year. Reuben was wont to walk about the neighborhood, and one afternoon he was found dead by the roadside, about a quarter of a mile from the house, on the main road. He was probably buried in the Cedar Swamp

THAYER.

burying ground, on the road from Ekonk to Sterling Hill. In June, 1776, he served a few days in Captain Belcher's company of Massachusetts militia. In 1777 he served five months in the Continental army.

CALEB THAYER, son of Reuben and Sarah (Linfield) Thayer, was born at Randolph, Mass., August 5, 1771, and January 3, 1796, married Rebecca Tillotson, who died July 8, 1804. He settled, either before or soon after her death, upon a farm of 200 acres about a mile east of Ekonk. in the town of Sterling, Conn., where, June 13, 1813, he married, for his second wife, Patience Phillips, daughter of Thomas and Catherine (Johnson) Phillips, of Coventry, R. I. The farm is situated at the end of lane running south and east about a quarter of a mile from the road going from Ekonk to Oneco, via Cedar Swamp burying ground. The house was situated on the brow of a hill which sloped to the north and east, and the foundation to the old house and some of the stepping stones leading to the well were still to be seen in 1892. In 1834 or thereabouts the old house was torn down and a new one built a few feet to the southeast of the old one, a portion of which formed the ell part of the new. About 300 feet west of the house and on the north side of the lane, near a brook, was situated a distillery, a portion of the foundation of which still remains. By whom this distillery was built is uncertain, but there is a legend concerning it which probably has some foundation in fact. It is said a young man was found dead, one morning, between the house and the distillery. It is supposed in climbing over a pair of bars he fell and broke his neck during the night. The farm has since run down till now (1894) it scarcely keeps three head of cattle.

In his old age, Caleb Thayer was very agreeable, and during his second wife's last illness he was especially kind to her. It is said after the death of his first wife he courted a young girl who finally became so in love with him that she

THAYER.

afterwards attempted suicide by hanging. In 1840 he removed to Hillsboro, Ohio, where, at the age of 70, he married a third wife. He died August 9, 1855, and was buried at Hillsboro. The old family Bible, bought in 1791, containing many valuable records, is still in the possession of the writer. In July, 1892, the writer took a bicycle trip from Hartford to Sterling, an account of which follows:

"Climbing up a long hill to Sterling Hill late one afternoon, I asked an old lady whom I met if she knew where the old Caleb Thayer farm was. I wanted to find the place where my father was born, and, if possible, sleep that night in the old homestead. In a town eight or ten miles square, I knew this was not an easy task. She knew nothing of such a place, but perhaps Tom Winsor could remember. She would go over and ask him. So we went across the road. Tom was a short, thickset, rough looking old man, 88 years of age. Naturally one would think he could remember back sixty years, for then it was that the farm passed out of the family name into other hands, whose, I know not. He hobbled slowly out to the fence where I stood holding the machine.

"'What under God's heaven you got there?' he said by way of preface. I told him briefly and then changed the subject and repeated the question I had asked the old lady. No, he could not remember or did not seem to care. Then I told him Fannie Thayer had lived on the farm a few years after my grandfather died. She was my aunt; did he remember her?

"'Fan Thayer your aunt,' he replied, waking up. 'The devil you say. Why, Fan Thayer's brother married my half sister. You see there were thirty-seven of us children, three crops, and she belonged to the last litter. Who was your father?' he demanded somewhat emphatically. I told him.

"'Gosh! I used to know Wales Thayer, and I always rather liked the darned old critter, too. I never knew anything bad of him. Come in and take supper and let's talk it over. Come in and stay over night,' and he started for the house.

(117)

THAYER.

"But I told him I wanted to find the old farm; could he tell me where it was? I thought sure one who remembered the old folks so well would know just where the old farm was, and blessed my good luck in finding out so easy. 'Do you remember where the old farm is?' I urged again and again, while he kept talking about everything else. It was getting late and I was getting anxious. Every minute I was afraid the old man would drop dead on the spot with apoplexy or something, and then all trace of the old place would be obliterated forever. Finally he said:

"'Why, yes, I remember where the old farm was,' and I held my breath. 'You go down to the old blacksmith's shop and turn to your right, and go on down to—you go down to— I can't remember—the devil, I can't remember nothing,' and with that the old man swore a blue streak for about five minutes. Much as he had forgotten, swearing was not one of his lost arts. He included in his remarks the house he lived in, the food he had to eat, the fence he was leaning on, and about everything but his wife. She, good woman, tried to pacify him and bring him back to the subject, but it was no use, and so I had to leave him.

"Bound to follow out the slightest clue, I turned south by the old blacksmith's shop and kept inquiring. One farmer thought they might have lived on a cross-road about two miles below there (a very reasonable supposition, I was willing to admit), and another was sure they never lived in Sterling at all. Finally, I got track of another old resident, Jim Curtis, over 90 years of age. He didn't know much, they said, but I thought, however much or little, it was more than I knew about the old farm.

"So I knocked at the door where he lived and found he had gone to bed. But I must see him. So the woman he lived with woke him up, and I asked him the same old question.

"'What do you want to know for?' he demanded gruffly,

THAYER.

raising himself on one elbow in bed, with his long white beard flowing down over his breast. I explained as well as I could. 'The old Cale Thayer farm? Why, anybody knows where the old Cale Thayer farm is,' and with that he lay down to sleep again. That would never do, for it was getting dark outside, and I must find the place. So we stirred him up again. 'The old Cale Thayer farm? Why, it is down on the Line Meeting-house road. Everybody down that way will tell you where it is,' and that was all we could get out of him. He seemed to think all the early settlers in that section were still alive and I could inquire of them.

"Just then I happened to remember that the old house was said to have been situated off the road up the end of a lane, perhaps half a mile, and I told the woman so. She said the Congdons had lived down the road on such a farm, and she thought they lived there now, but it was with faint hope that I started on again. Down a long hill I went, bumping over big boulders in the road and plowing through occasional sand, along the deep ruts and into a dark, dismal swamp. About two miles from this last house, in climbing a hill up out of the woods, I noticed in the dark a big, old-fashioned swing gate nailed up with boards. Here, certainly was a lane. So I worked the machine through the gate as well as I could and started up the narrow road, overgrown with bushes on either side as it was. Around a bend in the road I saw a light ahead. Here surely was a house, and in a short time I was knocking at the kitchen door.

"'I guess I have come on a fool's errand,'" I said, 'but I am trying to find where my father was born. His father used to live somewhere in the town of Sterling, and his name was Caleb Thayer.'

"'This is the place,' quickly piped up a female voice in-side. 'This is the old Cale Thayer farm,' she said, and then I was happy.

"The next day it punctured the poetry of the trip a little

(119)

to learn that the old house had been torn down years ago, and the present one was built a few feet away from the old foundation; but the ell part was the same, and the old farm was there, rocks and all. I stayed there two nights."

Hon. John W. Thayer, son of Caleb and Patience (Phillips) Thayer and father of the writer, was born at Sterling, Conn., December 25, 1819. Receiving a common-school education, he began the trade of wool sorter, and, after working at one or two other places, finally took a contract at Waterford, Mass., where he met Adaline Burton, daughter of Raymond and Deborah (Sayles) Burton. They were married, April 2, 1843, at the Free Will Baptist Church, in Waterford, the Rev. Maxy Burlingame officiating. The next day they started overland for Rockville, Conn., where he had entered into a business arrangement with the New England Company, one of the woolen manufacturing concerns of that place. The journey occupied two days, undertaken in a sleigh, but ending on wheels. From the position of wool sorter he soon rose to be superintendent of the New England Company, filling that position successfully several years. In 1860 he bought the Ellington mills, situated on the Hockanum river, about two miles west of Rockville, together with the tenements connected with the mill, and about fifty acres of land. He soon built a number of cottages for the employés, beautified the village in many ways, and named it Windermere, from Lake Windermere, in the lake regions of England. In July, 1861, while the mill was running day and night making army blankets, the two upper stories of the five were destroyed one night by fire, involving a heavy loss upon the company. A few years later the picker house was destroyed by fire. Notwithstanding these and other reverses, his management of the concern was so successful that his stock in the Windermere Woolen Company was at one time worth $100,000.

He early took an interest in military affairs. In 1856 he

THAYER.

was appointed adjutant of the Fifth regiment, state militia. In 1857 he was chosen major, in 1858 lieutenant-colonel, and in 1860 he was elected colonel of the same regiment, the last two commissions being signed by William A. Buckingham, afterwards the "War Governor" of Connecticut. In politics he was a Republican from the first. In 1855 he was elected to the House of Representatives from Rockville (town of Vernon) as a Know-Nothing. In 1865 he was again elected to the house, this time from the town of Ellington, a Democratic stronghold. In 1871 he was nominated for the senate from the 20th district, heretofore a Democratic one, and, after a lively contest, was elected by forty majority. He also held many minor town offices.

He was a great lover of music, studying and understanding it thoroughly. He taught singing in his native town when a very young man, and continued these "singing schools" at Waterford and after his settlement at Rockville. Upon coming to the latter place he at once took charge of the church singing, leading the choirs at the First and later the Second Congregational Churches for seventeen consecutive years, and first introducing instrumental music in church service. He was also captain of Talcott's Fifth regiment band for many years. The "Old Folks'" concerts were a feature of his work in the field of music at Rockville, these performances becoming famous all over the State.

In 1872, after several years of struggle against the grip which his commission merchants, Jordan, Marsh & Co., of Boston, had secured upon the mill property by questionable methods, he sold out his interest in the Windermere Woolen Company to them, and the next spring returned to Rockville. The long-continued mental strain resulted in nervous prostration, and treatment in the Connecticut Hospital for the Insane, at Middletown, was thought advisable. In a few months he had recovered completely, and was appointed supervisor of the institution. In a short time he was made clerk, a position

(121)

requiring the financial oversight of a community of 1,500 people and involving an outlay of $1,000 a day. This position he retained till his death. The hold which he gained upon the affections of the physicians and attendants of the institution was shown by their setting apart a day, after his death, for planting trees about the beautiful grounds in memory of him. The landscape gardening around the institution was the result of his fine taste and oversight. He also instituted a system of out-door exercise for the patients, which resulted in much good to them and caused the board of trustees officially to commend it in their reports. He died, March 19, 1889, and lies buried in Grove Hill cemetery, at Rockville.

Colonel Thayer, in his business relations, was the soul of honor, and in public affairs a leading spirit in the community. In his acquaintances he condescended to men of low degree, and in the bonds of friendship drew others to him with life-long attachments. He hated hypocrisy in every form, and strove to be estimated himself only for what he was. Pope was his favorite author. He early accepted the conclusions arrived at in Darwin's "Origin of Species," and when the book appeared, discussed the new doctrine with others in a way to leave a favorable and lasting impression on the young mind of the writer. In his home he was kind and affectionate, though of a highly-sensitive temperament, indulgent, and ever planning to make that home a happy one. That he was entirely successful will be seen in the story accompanying these sketches of a Christmas Eve at Windermere.

Tingley.

EPHRAIM TINGLEY, of Coventry, R. I., died at that place in July, 1776. His wife was Hannah (——). By his will he gave to his daughter, Elizabeth, $35 and "privilege in the house for a home so long as she lived single."

ELIZABETH TINGLEY, daughter of Ephraim and Hannah (——) Tingley, was born, probably, at Coventry, R. I., about 1735, and married Ebenezer Johnson, son of Elisha and Deborah (Sherman) Johnson, of Coventry, about 1760. She died at Coventry.

DESCENT.	Elizabeth Tingley	married	Ebenezer Johnson;
whose daughter,	Catherine Johnson,	"	Thomas Phillips;
" "	Patience Phillips,	"	Caleb Thayer;
whose son,	John W. Thayer,	"	Adaline Burton.

Tower.

ROBERT TOWER, father of one of the early Massachusetts settlers of that family name, lived in the parish of Hingham, County of Norfolk, England, where he married Dorothy Damon, August 31, 1607. He died at Hingham, May 1, 1634. His wife, Dorothy Damon, died at the same place, November 10, 1620.

JOHN TOWER, son of Robert and Dorothy (Damon) Tower, was born in the parish of Hingham, County of Norfolk, England, May 17, 1609, and came to this country early in the settlement of the Massachusetts colony. He settled at Hingham, in 1637, and February 13, 1638-9, married Margaret Ibrook, daughter of Richard Ibrook, at Charlestown, Mass. During the King Philip war he was often called upon to perform some hazardous duty, his friends saying, "You go, old John Tower, the Indians all know you and they won't hurt you."

He died at Hingham, February 13, 1701-2. The old Tower homestead was on Main street, next door south of the garrison house, near Tower bridge, in South Hingham.

IBROOK TOWER, son of John and Margaret (Ibrook) Tower, was born at Hingham, Mass., February 7, 1643-4, and married Margaret Hardin, daughter of John Hardin, of Braintree, April 24, 1668. He was by trade a cooper, and filled various town offices. His first wife, who was born in 1647, died at Hingham, November 19, 1705. His second wife was Patience (——). He died at Hingham, November 22, 1732, and in his will discharged his daughter, Esther, from all book debts.

(124)

TOWER.

ESTHER TOWER, daughter of Ibrook and Patience (——)
Tower, was born at Hingham, Mass., and married Morris
Tucker, son of John and Abigail (Hearnden) Tucker, of Providence, R. I., April 2, 1741. They settled at Burrillville, R. I.,
where she probably died.

DESCENT.	Esther Tower	married	Morris Tucker;
whose daughter,	Barbery Tucker,	"	Jeremiah Irons;
"	" Lillis Irons,	"	Arnold Sayles;
"	" Deborah Sayles,	"	Raymond Burton;
"	' Adaline Burton,	"	John W. Thayer.

Tucker.

MORRIS TUCKER, father of a noted Indian fighter, when he first came to this country, settled at Salisbury, Mass. His first wife was Elizabeth Stevens, who died October 16, 1662. His second wife was Elizabeth (——), by whom he had several children. It is believed he moved some years after to Providence, R. I., where he died, September 23, 1711.

JOHN TUCKER, son of Morris and Elizabeth (——) Tucker, is believed to be the famous Indian fighter, who came from the vicinity of Portsmouth, N. H., to Burrillville, R. I., late in the 17th century. He was born at Salisbury, Mass., August 16, 1664. In the journal kept by the Rev. John Pike, of Dover, N. H., who went to that frontier town in 1678, "for work of the ministry," is the following:

"July 26, 1696.—Sacrament Day. An ambush of Indians shot upon the poor people returning from meeting. Killed one man, two women, wounded three, and took John Tucker and two others."

A tradition of the family is that, escaping from the Indians, he was followed from Maine to Rhode Island by them, seeking revenge. While living at Burrillville he made a trip to New-York state, but soon returned. He was once nursed by an Indian squaw during a fit of sickness, from which doubtless arose the legend that he married her. Another legend connected with his career is one regarding his splitting rails out in the woods one day. While at work two Indians suddenly came upon him with their guns leveled at his head. He was unarmed, but finally persuaded them to spare his life till he had finished splitting the rail he was at work upon. During the operation he induced them to put their fingers in the crack and help to pry open the log, whereupon he knocked the iron wedge out

TUCKER.

and caught them fast. Then with their own guns he soon dispatched them both. He lived in the town of Burrillville many years, and died May 24, 1748–9. His grave, in 1894, with several others, could be found about 300 feet east of Sucker brook, near and on the west side of the highway between Chepachet and Mapleville. His wife was Abigail Hearnden, daughter of William and Esther (——) Hearnden, of Providence.

MORRIS TUCKER, son of John and Abigail (Hearnden) Tucker, was born probably at Providence, R. I., and was married to Esther Tower, daughter of Ibrook and Patience (——) Tower, the ceremony being performed by William Arnold, of Smithfield, April 2, 1741. He afterwards removed to Burrillville, where he probably died.

BARBERY TUCKER, daughter of Morris and Esther (Tower) Tucker, was born at Burrillville, R. I., in 1754, and married Captain Jeremiah Irons, son of Jeremiah and Bethiah (Dyer) Irons, of Burrillville, about 1774. She was described to the writer as a woman with a fair, plump, frank face, with blue eyes and small of stature. Whatever her husband lacked in the faculty for governing children she readily supplied, and a certain oxgoad was frequently brought into use in disciplining her offspring. Still, her descendants remember her as a woman with a pleasant disposition. She and her husband removed to Chepachet, where, many years after, she died, February 18, 1832. She lies buried beside her husband, in the back part of the old burying ground on the "Plains," between Chepachet and Mapleville.

DESCENT.	Barbery Tucker married	Jeremiah Irons;
whose daughter,	Lillis Irons,	" Arnold Sayles;
" "	Deborah Sayles,	" Raymond Burton;
" "	Adaline Burton,	" John W. Thayer.

(127)

Westcott.

STUKELEY WESTCOTT, one of the first settlers at Providence and a prominent citizen of Rhode Island for many years, was born in England in 1592, probably in Devonshire. He came to this country in 1636 with his wife and eight children and first settled at Salem, Mass., where, however, he was allowed to remain but a year or two. In March, 1638, he and several others were ordered by the General Court to remove out of the jurisdiction of the Massachusetts Bay colony and "great censure was passed upon them" by the Salem church. The next October, he and the other noteworthy eleven, received a deed of land at Providence from Roger Williams, who, in turn, had but recently purchased it from the Indians. The First Baptist Church was organized at Providence this year with Stukeley Westcott as one of the original members. In 1640, he signed the civil compact with thirty-eight others. Eight years later, in 1648, he had removed to Warwick, still retaining his real estate at Providence. In 1651, the town council ordered "the ditch which Stukeley Westcott made upon the street shall stand, being about three or four pole, having paid his fine to the town which he was fined." Being, for many years, a surveyor of highways, in 1652 he and two others were appointed to lay out the meadows about the town "for the inhabitants which are yet not provided for and so it is to be cast lot for." In 1653 he was on a committee to confer with the Indians about fencing, etc. In 1655 he and another were ordered "to cast up what damage is due to the Indians and place every man's share according to his proportion and gather it up and in case any one refuse to pay upon demand then it shall be taken by distress." In 1660, as foreman of a "Grand Inquest," he rendered a verdict, "we who are engaged to see the dead Indian, do find

(128)

by diligent search that he was beaten, which was the cause of his death." Twice he was appointed to keep an "ordinary" for the entertainment of strangers during the time the king's commissioners held court in Warwick and a sign was to be set out in "the most perspicuous" place. The town council frequently met at his house and he served five times as commissioner. He was twice an assistant and eight times a deputy. In 1672 he and his sons were among the earliest to sign a compact to resist the encroachments of the Connecticut authorities on Rhode Island territory. During the King Philip war one of his sons was killed and the others finally fled to the Island of Prudence where they could raise a crop for themselves in safety. Stukeley, now eighty-four years of age and wifeless, was driven for refuge to the island of Rhode Island, where, at Portsmouth, at the home of his grandson, Caleb Arnold, he soon failed in health and died, January 12, 1677. Upon the day of his death he made his will, but was requested by his grandson not to sign it till his (Stukeley's) sons from Prudence Island could be sent for. When they arrived he was unable to write and died in a short time. The will was finally substantially approved by the town council. Stukeley Westcott's farm was about a mile and a half northwest of Rocky Point, at the intersection of what is now known as Sandy Lane in Old Warwick and the old post road now known as Main street, running westerly to Apponaug. The farm was situated in the southwest corner of these two roads. In England, before coming to this country, Stukeley Westcott was known as a Separatist. The name of his wife or the date of their marriage can not be given.

JEREMIAH WESTCOTT, youngest son of Stukeley Westcott, was born in England, probably in Devonshire, and came to this country in 1636 with his father when quite young. Upon the final settlement of his father at Warwick, R. I., Jeremiah, in 1665, July 27, married Eleanor England, daughter of

WESTCOTT.

William and Elizabeth (——) England, of Portsmouth, R. I. In 1664 he was appointed an officer of the town to take an Indian prisoner to Newport. In 1666 he was chosen a committee to warn the Indians not to plant on town lands. He always lived on his father's farm, and in 1686 died, leaving no will. The town council therefore made one for him.

WILLIAM WESTCOTT, son of Jeremiah and Eleanor (England) Westcott, was born at Warwick, R. I., about 1680, and married Abigail Gardiner, probably daughter of George and Tabitha (Tefft) Gardiner of Kings Town. About 1700 he moved from Warwick to Cranston, where he bought a farm of 1,000 acres. It was located about a mile south of Knightsville, on the east side of the road, about half a mile from the bridge over the New England railroad. In 1894 an immense stone wall had been built along the highway directly in front of the site of the old homestead. All that remained was the well, the foundation stones of the cellar, the stump of an old cedar tree referred to in the deeds dated 1732 and 1805 and several uninscribed graves. Doubtless they are those of William Westcott and several of his descendants. He died in 1758 or not long after.

CAPTAIN WILLIAM WESTCOTT, son of William and Abigail (Gardiner) Westcott, was born probably at Cranston, R. I., about 1700–5. He was admitted freeman in 1730 and in 1733 was appointed constable. He was twice married, his first wife being Katherine (——) and his second Joanna (——), who died June 10–1809. He always lived, and finally died in January, 1781, at Cranston, on the old homestead, a part of which farm his father gave him.

ALICE WESTCOTT, daughter of Captain William and Katherine (——) Westcott, was born at Cranston, R. I., about

WESTCOTT.

1730–5 and married Benjamin Burton, son of William and Persis (Burlingame) Burton, of Cranston, December 25, 1755. She died, probably, at Cranston.

DESCENT.	Alice Westcott	married	Benjamin Burton;
whose son,	Edmond Burton,	"	Lucretia Boardman;
" "	Raymond "	"	Deborah Sayles;
" daughter,	Adaline "	"	John W. Thayer.

Whipple.

JOHN WHIPPLE, one of those in Rhode Island "who staid and went not away" during the King Philip war, was born in England about 1617, possibly the son of Matthew Whipple, a clothier, of Bocking, Essex County. Upon coming to this country, he first settled at Dorchester, Mass. In 1632, while yet a lad, he is on record in that town as being ordered to give his master, Israel Stoughton, "for wasteful expenditure of powder and shot," three shillings and fourpence. In 1639 he married Sarah (——), who was but 15 years old, and two years later they joined the church. He was a carpenter by trade, and his farm of fifty acres was the present location of Neponset Village. In 1658 he sold his farm and removed to Providence, R. I., where, for seven years, he was chosen deputy. In 1674, he was licensed to "keep an ordinary." During the King Philip war he "staid and went not away," and so shared in the disposition of the captive Indians whose services were sold to those plucky inhabitants for a term of years. He died, May 16, 1685, and, with his wife, Sarah, who died in 1666, was first buried on his own land, but subsequently their remains were removed to the North Burial Ground, in Providence. His house stood a little north of Star street, between North Main and Benefit streets, and was standing as late as 1780 or 1800.

ELEAZER WHIPPLE, a soldier in the King Philip war, during which he was wounded, was born at Dorchester, Mass., March 8, 1646, and came to Providence, R. I., with his father, at the age of 12 years. He married Alice Angell, daughter of Thomas and Alice (——) Angell, of Providence, January 26, 1669. He was a housewright by trade, and was twice appointed deputy. During the King Philip war he was wounded,

(132)

WHIPPLE.

the town holding his receipt for £6, the amount it paid him "for his curing." He died, August 25, 1719, leaving an estate valued at nearly £500.

HANNAH WHIPPLE, daughter of Eleazer and Alice (Angell) Whipple, was born at Providence, R. I., March 5, 1695, and married William Arnold, son of John and Mary (Mowry) Arnold, of Smithfield, December 27, 1717. They lived at Smithfield, where she doubtless died.

DESCENT.	Hannah Whipple married William Arnold;
whose daughter,	Martha Arnold,	"	John Sayles;
" son,	Ishmael Sayles,	"	Deborah Aldrich;
" "	Arnold "	"	Lillis Irons;
" daughter,	Deborah "	"	Raymond Burton;
" "	Adaline Burton,	"	John W. Thayer.

Whipple.

JONATHAN WHIPPLE, by whom, it is recorded, a wolf's head was brought in that he had "killed not far of the town," one day in his sixteenth year, was born in Providence, R. I., in 1664, the son of John and Sarah (——) Whipple. He married Margaret Angell, daughter of Thomas and Alice (——) Angell, of Providence, about 1687. She died about 1700, and for his second wife he married Anne (——), who survived him two years. He died at Providence, September 8, 1721.

SARAH WHIPPLE, daughter of Jonathan and Margaret (Angell) Whipple, was born at Providence, R. I., about 1688, and married Samuel Irons, probably son of Samuel and Sarah (Belcher) Irons, of Braintree, Mass., May 3, 1709. They lived at Providence, where she doubtless died.

DESCENT.	Sarah Whipple,	married	Samuel Irons;
whose son,	Jeremiah Irons,	"	Bethiah Dyer;
" "	" "	"	Barbery Tucker;
" daughter,	Lillis "	"	Arnold Sayles;
" "	Deborah Sayles,	"	Raymond Burton;
" "	Adaline Burton,	"	John W. Thayer.

White.

WILLIAM WHITE, whose letter to Governor John Winthrop, in 1648, bears indications of being written by a man of considerable practical scientific knowledge, came from Derbyshire, England, about 1645, under contract to work for one Doctor Child, of Boston. Becoming dissatisfied in a short time, he departed from Boston, but his letter to Governor Winthrop best tells the reasons why: "I desire to give your worship a touch of the causes of my passage, howe first I was promised 5s. a day by Doctor Child for myselfe and my sonn and two cows and house rent free and land for me and all my children, also covenant for the same. But they deffered the covenants and I never had them nor performance, to my great loose and, if you knew all, a greater loose to the covenanter. I should have come over about the tyme that Mr. John Wenthropp cam over. If I had the iron mynes of Newe Ingland had been tryed with less cost, for I tryed most of the mynes in Derbasharre with a bloom harth. I told Mr. Doctor Child more of the Nehaunte myne than I can now spick of. For most parte of the York mynes, they lye at the day and are partly cutt from their life and the speritt of feusion and sollidditie is not in them. But the swomp myne is living and good. Great riches concerning whit glass and two other things not to be spoken of, are within four miles of Boston. More at large I will write when it shall please God that I write the good news from Bermoodos. It may please God I may see you next springe for there is greate things for me to doe. The second cause is longe, strong winter. 3 cause, the base disaster of strong Furnald's wife against my poore harmless wiffe. 4thly, the countrie pay is bad to get when a poore man hath earned it that it comes to little or nothing. 5, being now * * all things prevaile against me. 6, I see such hard dealings with shop-keepers both

(185)

WHITE.

in price, weight and measure and they professe much and also such sewing one another in courts that I think love is wantinge which is the main key of religion, for without love it is nothinge. More I have to say but not this time." Written "from abord the Returne."

Instead of going to the Bermudas, it is believed he settled for a time at Providence, where he bought a house and lot. He and his wife, Elizabeth, returned to Boston in 1654, and in 1662 sold their house and lot in Providence to their daughter, Elizabeth Hearnden. Her parents, probably both, died in Boston.

ELIZABETH WHITE, daughter of William and Elizabeth (——) White, was probably born in England, about 1630, and came to this country soon after with her parents. About 1650 she married Benjamin Hearnden, of Providence, R. I. who died in 1687. She then married Richard Pray, whom she also survived. She died at Providence in 1701 or soon after.

DESCENT.	Elizabeth White	married	Benjamin Hearnden;
whose son,	William Hearnden,	"	Esther (——);
" daughter,	Abigail "	"	John Tucker;
" son,	Morris Tucker,	"	Esther Tower;
" daughter,	Barbery "	"	Jeremiah Irons;
" "	Lillis Irons,	"	Arnold Sayles;
" "	Deborah Sayles,	"	Raymond Burton;
" "	Adaline Burton,	"	John W. Thayer.

Wickes.

John Wickes, one of the Gorton party at Warwick, R. I., to suffer from the action of the Massachusetts troops and magistrates in 1643 and destined to finally have his head set upon a stake in front of his own house in 1676, was born at Staines, Middlesex County, England, in 1609. He sailed with his wife, Mary, and daughter in the ship "Hopewell" from London in September, 1635, and first landed and settled at Plymouth, Mass. In 1639 he removed to Portsmouth, R. I. He was a tanner by trade. At first he seemed to be a disturbing element, for the General Court, in 1640, passed a vote that "if he come upon the island armed he shall, by the constable (calling to him sufficient aid) be disarmed and carried before the magistrate and there find surety for his good behavior; provided this order hinder not the course of law already begun with John Wickes." He was, however, one of the twenty-nine signers of the civil compact or form of government at Portsmouth. During a public trial of one of his friends, Wickes once made such a disturbance that an armed guard was called and suppressed him by putting him in the stocks.

In 1643 he and Sam Gorton, whose earliest disciple and companion he was, and ten others, for 144 fathoms of wampum bought of Miantinomo a tract of land at Warwick and settled there. In September of the same year the men of Warwick were summoned to appear at the General Court at Boston to hear complaints entered against them by two Indian sachems of unfair dealings towards them. The Warwickites declined to obey the summons, claiming they were beyond the jurisdiction of the Massachusetts court A body of troops were accordingly sent from Boston to Warwick, the town was besieged and the men were finally captured after their homes

(137)

had been burned down and their wives and children driven out into the woods.

In November, Wickes and the others of the Gorton party were brought before the General Court at Boston, charged with heresy and sedition. Wickes and others raised such a disturbance he was put in the stocks and finally was sent to Ipswich and confined in irons in prison during the pleasure of the court, with the additional penalty hanging over him that if he should break jail or preach his heresies or speak against the church or state, on conviction he should die. The following March he was released and banished both from Massachusetts and Warwick. Wickes soon returned to Warwick and held many public offices, including that of assistant for three years, commissioner for eight years and deputy for eleven years. In 1651 he and three others built a mill at their own expense for the privilege of grinding the town's corn for two quarts a bushel. In 1670 he and Groton, who with several others had soon returned to Warwick after their imprisonment at Boston, were imprisoned, the records say, for refusing to pay the old tax due by the town to the colony.

During the King Philip war, he then being a very ancient man, he was wont to answer the oft-repeated admonitions of his friends to be more careful of his safety by saying that he had no fears of injury from the Indians—they would not hurt him. From his past experience of their uniform kindness and good will towards him personally he was slow to believe himself in danger. With this mistaken confidence in their fidelity, he ventured beyond the protection of the garrison on March 17, 1675-6, and going at evening into the woods in search of his cows he never came back. His fate was first known to his friends the next morning on seeing his head set upon a pole near his own dwelling. This they immediately, and before venturing in search of his body, buried near the stone castle and within a few rods of it. The body, which was found upon the succeeding day, was buried beside the head, but in a distinct grave. The graves, with a number of others, were easily found by the writer in 1894 on the road to Apponaug, a short distance west of Old Warwick and north of Old Warwick Cove. The graves were in the rear of the George Anthony homestead on the north side of the road, in front of which was a handsome large elm.

The inscriptions over John Wickes' grave were as follows: " John Wickes, born 1609, Marie, his wife, born 1607 and his daughter, Anna, born 1634, came to New England, 1635. Hannah, their daughter, married William Burton, of Mashanticut, Cranston, R. I." Reverse side: " Here lie the remains of John Wickes, Esquire, born 1609, at Staines, England, came to New England, 1635, an original purchaser of Warwick, 1643. In Philip's Indian War, after the town was burnt, on going out from Thomas Greene's stone castle to look for his cattle on 17 March, 1675-6, he was slain by Indians and his head set on a pole." The foundation stones to the castle were still to be found near the graves. John Wickes' dwelling house, nothing of which remains, was on the corner leading to Rocky Point nearly opposite the old Quaker meeting-house and on the west side of the road.

MARY (——), his wife, was born in England in 1607, and was therefore twenty-eight years old when they came from England in 1635. In September, 1643, when the Massachusetts troops besieged the Warwick settlement and finally took the men captives, she and her four children, the oldest not ten years of age, were driven into the woods and that fall and the following winter were obliged to shift for themselves. Her husband was unable to return to her probably till 1646 when a royal command was issued permitting him and others to live at Warwick without molestation from Massachusetts.

HANNAH WICKES, daughter of John and Mary (——) Wickes, was born at Staines, Middlesex County, England, in

1634, and was brought to this country by her father at the age of one year. At the age of nine years, she with her mother and brother and two sisters, suffered from the siege of the Massachusetts troops at Warwick, R. I. In 1650–5 she married William Burton, of Cranston, and died about 1700.

DESCENT.	Hannah Wickes	married	William Burton;
whose son,	John Burton,	"	Mary (———);
" "	William Burton,	"	Persis Burlingame;
" "	Benjamin Burton,	"	Alice Westcott;
" "	Edmond "	"	Lucretia Boardman;
" "	Raymond "	"	Deborah Sayles;
" daughter,	Adaline "	"	John W. Thayer.

Wilkinson.

LIEUTENANT LAWRENCE WILKINSON was a defender of Charles I., fighting as a lieutenant in the Royal army. At the siege of Newcastle-upon-Tyne he was taken prisoner when the town fell into the hands of the Parliamentary army, October 22, 1644. His estate was thereupon sequestered and sold by order of Parliament. Having obtained special permission from Lord Fairfax, Lieutenant Wilkinson came, with his wife and son, to America. The records of 1645–47, at Durham, where the sequestration took place, have this: "Lawrence Wilkinson, of Lanchester, officer in arms, went to New England." He soon came to Providence, R. I., where, in 1657, land was granted him. In 1659 he served as juryman and commissioner, in 1667 as commissioner and deputy, and in 1673, again as deputy. He died at Providence, August 9, 1692. His wife was Susannah, daughter of Christopher and Alice (——) Smith, probably of Lanchester, England.

Lawrence Wilkinson was the son of William Wilkinson, of Lanchester, by his wife, Mary, sister of Sir John Conyers, Bart , and the grandson of Lawrence Wilkinson, of Harpsley House, county of Durham, to whom the family arms were confirmed and the crest granted, September 18, 1615.

JOHN WILKINSON, son of Lawrence and Susannah (Smith) Wilkinson, of Lanchester, England, was born probably at Providence, R. I., March 2, 1654, and married Deborah Whipple, April 16, 1689. During the King Philip war he was wounded, and the town, in 1682, voted him £10 in compensation for his injuries. In 1700, and again in 1706, he was chosen deputy. In the inventory of his estate were joiners', coopers' and carpenters' tools, and a "negro youth, £30." He died at Providence, April 10, 1708.

WILKINSON.

FREELOVE WILKINSON, daughter of John and Deborah (Whipple) Wilkinson, was born at Providence, R. I., June 25, 1701, and married Michael Phillips, son of James and Mary (Mowry) Phillips, of Providence. They removed to Smithfield about 1735, where she probably died.

DESCENT.	Freelove Wilkinson married Michael Phillips;
whose son,	James Phillips, " —— ——;
" "	Thomas " " Catherine Johnson;
" daughter,	Patience " " Caleb Thayer;
" son,	John W. Thayer, " Adaline Burton.

Williams.

JAMES WILLIAMS, father of Roger Williams, the founder of Rhode Island, was a merchant tailor in London, England. He was probably born at St. Albans, Hertfordshire, where, about 1590, he married Alice Pemberton, daughter of Robert and Catherine (——) Pemberton, of St. Albans, and soon after moved to and went into business at London. He died in November, 1621, leaving his property to his wife and children, among others, mentioning his son, Roger. He also made provisions for the distribution of money and bread among the poor of St. Sepulchres, without Newgate, on the day or day following his funeral.

ROGER WILLIAMS, founder of the Rhode Island colony, was the son of James and Alice (Pemberton) Williams, of London, England. He was born possibly at St. Albans, Hertfordshire, about 1599, where his parents lived for a short time after their marriage and before going to London. He was elected scholar and was sent to Sutton's Hospital, in 1621, by Sir Edward Coke, who took a liking to him from seeing him take sermons and speeches in the Star Chamber in shorthand. In 1625 he entered Pembroke College, Cambridge, and in 1627 took the degree of Bachelor of Arts. In 1629 he was chaplain to Sir William Masham, of Otes, in the parish of High Laver, in Essex County. In 1630, December 1, he embarked at Bristol in the ship, "Lion," and arrived at Boston, Mass., February 5, 1631. In a few weeks he was settled as pastor over the church at Salem, spending a part of the following summer, however, at Plymouth. In 1635. in the spring, he was summoned from Salem before the court at Boston for some offense in his preaching, and the following October he was banished from the colony. In January, 1636, the order of the court not having been obeyed, a messenger was sent to Salem to arrest him, when it was found he had fled three days before. In writing of his experience at that time, he said: "I was sorely tossed for one fourteen weeks in a bitter winter season, not knowing what bed and bread did mean." First seeking a settlement within the limits of the Plymouth colony, on Seekonk river, he was warned away, and finally came by water, with five companions in canoes, to the present site of Providence, R. I. This same year his mediations, at the request of Massachusetts, prevented a coalition of the Pequots with the Narragansetts and Mohegans. In writing of this service, years after, he said: "Three days and nights my business forced me to lodge and mix with the bloody Pequot ambassadors, whose hands and arms methought reeked with the blood of my countrymen murdered and massacred by them on Connecticut river." His interest in the colony and the important part he took in its affairs during the next half century, nearly, need not here be retold. These particulars are easily accessible in most public libraries. In 1682, when he was past four-score, he wrote: "I am old and weak and bruised (with rupture and colic), and lameness on both feet." He died in the spring of 1683, and was buried on his own land, northeast of the junction of Benefit and Bowen streets, Providence.

In digging a grave near his about 100 years after his death, a sexton obtained a view of his bones, which were then covered over completely with a long mossy substance. In 1860 a systematic effort was made to locate his grave, and, upon being successful, the party of investigators proceeded to make careful preparations toward removing his remains. Upon digging down to the known location of the head of the coffin the root of an adjacent apple tree was discovered. This tree had pushed downwards one of its main roots in a sloping direction and in nearly a straight course towards the precise spot that had been occupied by the skull of Roger Williams. There— making a turn conforming with the circumference of the skull—

the root followed the direction of the back bone to the hips, where it divided into two branches, each one following a leg bone to the heel, where they both turned upwards to the extremities of the toes of the skeleton. One of the roots formed a slight crook at the part occupied by the knee joint, thus producing an increased resemblance to the outline of the skeleton of Roger Williams. This root has been preserved, and was seen by the writer in 1894 in the museum at Brown University.

By the side of the grave of Roger Williams was another, supposed to be that of his wife, Mary. In this grave, wonderfully preserved, was found a lock of braided hair, the sole remaining human relic found in either grave, all else having completely disappeared.

The wife of Roger Williams is said to have been Mary Warnard. A possible clue to her identity is found in a letter of his written May 2, 1629, while he was chaplain to Sir William Masham, of Otes. Sir William had married a daughter of Sir Francis Barrington, and in writing to Lady Joan Barrington, after the death of Sir Francis, Roger expressed his affection for her niece.

MARY WILLIAMS, daughter of Roger and Mary (Warnard) Williams, was born at Salem, Mass., in August, 1633, and about 1650 married John Sayles, of Providence, R. I., son of John Sayles, formerly of Manchester, England. They lived at Providence, where she died in 1681. She was buried with her husband in the Easton burial ground, Middletown, near Sachuset Beach.

DESCENT.	Mary Williams	married	John Sayles;
whose son,	John Sayles,	"	Elizabeth Olney;
" "	Thomas "	"	Esther Scott;
" "	John "	"	Martha Arnold;
" "	Ishmael "	"	Deborah Aldrich;
" "	Arnold "	"	Lillis Irons;
" daughter,	Deborah "	"	Raymond Burton;
" "	Adaline Burton,	"	John W. Thayer.

(145)

Sunday at Windermere.

ONE SUNDAY in July, I visited Windermere, the home of my boyhood. Purposely I took a route through a section of country entirely new to me, but there was little risk of my getting lost, for, like a carrier pigeon, I was a homing boy once more, let loose from a trap of busy newspaper life, and could easily find my way back. How happy I was, gliding along through the woods on my pneumatic! The overhanging limbs and branches sprinkled me with their morning blessing; the smell of the woods and the new-made hay was incense to my soul; the blossoming chestnuts, swarming with chanting bees, filled the air with heavenly music, and even the bushes and barposts along the way, clutching at little clumps of hay, appeared to have received an offertory from every passing pilgrim. Every thought within me was a morning prayer.

But as my old home drew near the ideal gave way to the real, and all the little scrapes and difficulties I ever got into began to crowd themselves upon my memory. I was not a bad boy, as they run, neither was I a goody-goody boy, else I should not have lived to make this tricennial visit.

"I never whipped you at school but once," said my old school teacher, whom I happened to meet about a mile from Windermere, getting ready for church, "and afterwards I found out you were not to blame. You wouldn't tell on another boy and got the whipping yourself, instead of him." I had always remembered the occurrence distinctly, and never have forgotten that I had to go out and cut the very stick with which I was to be whipped. To have to do that was the unkindest cut of all. I remember, too, as I went blubbering around the school house, every switch I found seemed to be too big. But then, it did me some good now to have her acknowledge, after so many years, that she was wrong. If she had found out her mistake before the whipping, I should have liked it still better.

But if that was the only whipping I ever had at school, it was far from being the only one I ever had. One morning an indefinite impression took possession of me that I did not want to go to school. I had been sent over to the store for some sugar and knew I should be late—that I never was, and I didn't want to begin then, so I decided not to go. Mother reached an entirely different decision. Hers prevailed, but not till the case had been argued at considerable length—at arms' length most of the time. I started for school all right, but tried hiding behind a tree. She started for me and tried hiding, too. "No, Tom," once said Lord Macauley's mother, under a somewhat similar provocation, "if it rains cats and dogs, you shall go to school." He went—and so did I. Whether it rained cats and dogs in his case his biographer saith not, but in my case blow upon blow rained down upon my back, arms and legs, and the shower did not blow over till I finally entered the school-room door, half a mile distant. After school, that night, still intent upon gaining my point, I bravely bared my back and called mother's attention to the red ridges across it, in hopes of drawing out some expression of sorrow. While the sight caused my sister to cry sympathetically, mother never expressed—to me— the slightest regret, and her apparent indifference afterwards hurt worse than the original whipping. But I shall never get to Windermere, if I loiter by the way like this.

Well, then, after a delightful two hours' ride, I put my machine up in a barn near by and started down the road towards my old home, filled with the happiest anticipations. The barn, to be sure, recalled to my mind the robbery of some hens' nests there, some thirty years before, and the humiliating result, but that has all gone by now. There was nothing particularly clever about the theft that I remember. The eggs were in the nests and we took them, Tommy and I, that was all. Wandering over by the sandbank afterwards, in order to realize from the spoils, we mixed the eggs up into some mud pies. After they had been baked in the sun, I stumped Tommy to eat some of the sandy stuff, and we did taste of it a little. Had we shown grit enough to eat it, shells and all, and thus cover up our tracks, it would have been far, far better for me. As it was, the old lady, missing the customary supply at the barn, went hunting for her eggs, and over at the sandbank she found the missing shells and the remnants of a mock feast, and that night, before going to bed, I was moved to return to her nine eggs, and two or three extra ones to make sure. But what was worse, I had to tell her I was sorry. I was. I was awfully sorry—so sorry I cried some—but, like most criminals, I was sorry I got caught, that was all. I never was sorry about the eggs.

At last the old yellow brick house, where thirteen of the happiest years of my life were spent! To me every spear of grass, every foot of ground about the old place was sacred, and I approached it again, hoping others had as sacredly kept it. The large, handsome elm tree, with its branches bending to the ground, was still there, in the full vigor of its second century of life, but what was the matter with the house and its surroundings? The hitching post in front, on top of which I used to pile up the fragments of fire crackers for a light till they had burned a deep hole in the post, had long since rotted off and disappeared. The gate was still on its hinges, but it would not swing, the posts had inclined towards each other so, in one last embrace. I stepped into the yard, and "Trespassing forbidden on these grounds under penalty of the law," stared me in the face. The old doorstep, with a place on it worn smooth where I used to sharpen my slate pencils, had grown green with age and disuse. I tried the door. The knob remained wherever my friendly hand turned it, so rusty had it become. The door bell, too, came out without any response and stayed there, like a skeleton hand, to greet me. The blinds were closed, all those that were not broken or gone, and some of the large lights were broken out. Shut out at the door, I peeped in through one of the broken windows. A cold, musty draft of air came out, as if a dead person had breathed in my face. It chilled my home love. The rooms were empty, the floors were bare, excepting where the plastering had fallen down. There was the very spot where at night I used to lie down under the table and go to sleep, and there was where the sofa stood from which I always woke up in time for the apples and cider. How many times, for hours and hours, have I gone around those rooms on my hands and knees, building forts out of dominoes, and gunboats and rebel rams out of clothes pins, and manning them with small copper pennies, the red ones for rebels and the lighter-colored ones representing the Union army. Every penny was a thousand men, and during some naval battle, such as the capture of Fort Jackson and Fort Phillip, below New Orleans, which I fought out over and over again, it was no uncommon thing to lose 1,000 men overboard at a clip. Then, during the Wilderness campaign, with one hand I often turned Lee's flank, and with two hands easily put 10,000 men to flight. Occasionally hostilities would be suspended for a time, owing to the fact that some member of the family who wore long dresses had just passed hurriedly through the room. The strongest fortress would then be laid low and the warships dismasted by the hurricane, and with great loss of life swept out to sea. I never could successfully explode the mine at Petersburg, but all the rest of that struggle, around to Five Forks and Appomattox, was fought out to perfection, time and again. But the war is over now, and those battlefields that were then strewn thick with the mangled bodies of thousands of brave men, who willingly gave up their lives that their country might live, every time a rainy day came and I couldn't go to school, are now covered with plastering, wall paper and the dust of years.

I went around to the west side of the house. The walls had bulged out and were braced up with heavy sticks of timber

Decomposition had surely set in, and the house, my dear old home, had begun to bloat. I tried every window. The blinds were nailed up and the windows nailed down. How I longed to get in. But I must get a look anyhow at my old bedroom window on the north side of the house. There it was, smashed in. Surely I could never sleep there now, although I used to with the fine snow sifting in through the cracks and falling upon my sleeping face. One look into the old kitchen! "Now there will be a war." How little I realized what that meant, but I shall never forget how mother looked and where she stood on that kitchen floor when she said it. Lincoln, the day before, had been elected the first time and we had just heard the news. How the sight of that room brought it all back in an instant. I walked away a short distance to see how the home looked as a whole. Still worse. The chimneys were tumbling in; the shingles were falling off. Oh, I didn't like to see it. It made me sick. My old home was dead, dead forever to me. Let me get away. I went out back of the house to the canal. That too was empty. In it was no water, no life. The flume was there, just a semblance of it, but where was the little willow twig that once saved my life. Not a sign of it. Who could have cut that down? Who could have been so mean? But what of the twig? This: One morning, in running across the stick of timber at the head of the flume, my foot slipped and I went in, over my head. The sides of the flume were boarded up, and I remember as I came up that my bare feet could get no hold on the slimy boards and I went under again. The second time up I grabbed some of the long grass on the side of the bank, but that too gave way and let me under again. It was quite a distance from the house, and if I yelled no one heard me. I don't suppose I did, but this I do remember: In coming up the last time, I caught hold of a little willow twig growing on the edge of the flume, and that did not give way. The next I remember I was going into the house crying and dripping from head to foot. That is why I looked for the

(150)

\

little willow twig, but when I stopped to consider that this was over thirty years ago, the chances are the twig that saved my life grew to a tree and has since been cut down. The stick of timber and the slimy boards too are gone, and nothing remains but a few loose stones to even mark the spot. Should these crumble away and disappear, the event itself will still ever remain fixed in my memory. Near by, however, was the old tree with the iron ring driven into it, to which so many times I had tied up the old, leaky, flat-bottom boat. Further along was the very spot, now dry and sandy, where once I had successfully launched several wash tubs, the property of an old German woman living close by who took in washing. The wind blew off shore, I remember, and bore the tubs away, much to my intense delight, clear across the pond. Later, much to my intense anguish, I also remember having my ear energetically pulled for thus building up a navy at the old woman's expense, but this should be said in mitigation of father's action—it was the nearest approach to a whipping he ever gave me.

The old pig pen, near the barn, had not entirely disappeared, but the two pet pigs, Patrick and Bridget Murphy by name, had. That is, as pigs they had. We used to hold them in our laps till they grew so heavy we couldn't lift them, all at once, and then we put them away in a barrel that held them, and we lifted them out a piece at a time. In passing, this bit of an obituary is due them. Our pets were many, and the wild as well as domesticated ones were made to submit, but of all the well-behaved pets we ever kept—horses, dogs, cats, crows, lambs, turtles and snakes—those pet pigs were the only ones, when urged to change their form of living, that, like Jeshurun, waxed fat and kicked. It stuck in their throats to die, so we let them live, in us, and they have ever since dwelt in our memories

Along the banks of the old pond I had watched the little "pumpkin seeds" in their watery nests for hours, and occasion- ·

ally, by slipping my hook under his jaw, I had yanked up big bull frog. Recalling this and much more, I came to another spot made historic by an event, the cause of which has hitherto remained a mystery to everyone but myself, and is now divulged for the first time.

In carrying out one of my engineering schemes, I had dug a small trench through the bank of the pond to let the water into a system of miniature canals and water wheels I had constructed on the lower side of the bank. These canals at different levels furnished power for several important manufacturing concerns, which were a source of great pride but little revenue to me. One night I was called away suddenly to go on an errand, and left the wheels running, intending to return later in the evening and shut down for the night. Something came up, however, to divert my mind from the cares of business, and I forgot all about my water wheels and went to bed. During the night the pond rose, the water gradually increased the size of the trench, and about 4 o'clock the next morning finally swept the entire bank away. Besides practically obliterating one of the most complete systems of canals I had ever constructed, the break in the bank *incidentally* drew the pond off, stopped a large cotton batting mill from running, threw some thirty or forty hands out of employment, and caused damage to the amount of several hundred dollars. The mill owners and everyone concerned wondered how it could have happened, and do wonder to this day, but I don't.

Just beyond I came to the outlet of the pond, a stream usually dry in the daytime when the mill was running, but acting as an overflow for the surplus water at night. How many suckers and eels I have caught with my hands, wading up and down this brook! Yes, there is the identical bog and overhanging bank where I came near catchin_ something else one day. The water was up to my knees, I remember, and my sleeves were rolled up, and I was slyly reaching in under the bank for the good sized sucker I had seen live under there,

hen my hand came in contact with a monstrous snapping tur-
.e. Lucky for me, in feeling around under the bank, I got
hold of his tail instead of his head, or I might not be holding
this pen between my fingers so easily. As it was, I let go and
got out of that hole about as quick as any boy ever did, and
stayed out too for one while. But now there was no water, no
turtle, nothing but turf and grass, and the very course of a
stream once so full of interest to me was almost obliterated by
the years of pasturing for which the land had been used.
Speaking of turtles, we caught one once that was able to walk
away with me on his back. I had, time and again, at low water,
waded about the pond till the little blood-suckers between my
toes or a broken bottle under my foot had made the water red
with blood, and had poled the leaky old boat about for hours
at a time, but now all was dry pasture land and had been for
years. The pond itself had now shrunken away to a mere mud
hole.

Leaving the few scattered descendants remaining of the
once flourishing colony of muskrats inhabiting that region, I
started off across the lots towards the old spring, half a mile
distant. At last there was a familiar sound. That same old
red-winged blackbird, or if not the original, one just like him,
that I had pegged stones at so many times going through the
tall meadow grass thirty odd years ago, immediately recognized
and began to dive down at me with a courage, apparently born
of a knowledge, either of my former poor markmanship or my
present more kindly disposition. No bird, ignorant of these
traits of mine, would have taken such chances as this one did,
but I let him dive and went on. There was the same path
through the grass, the same bogs covered with wintergreen,
apparently the same cows that used to chase Bruiser out of the
lot. Here, however, was something new lying in the grass, a
cigarette package, empty, of course. Thirty years ago that
surely was not there. There were no cigarettes then, but let
no one be deceived for a moment by thinking we boys didn't

smoke on the sly, just the same then as they do now. There were lots of moss and plenty of dry grape vines, and many a rattan hoop skirt have I hidden away and secretly smoked up. They may have their cigarettes if they want to, but I tell you the boys nowadays, since crinoline went out of fashion, don't have hoop skirts to smoke as I did. Occasionally I got hold of a cigar or a cigar stump, and that reminds me how that sin once found me out. I had been up to the fair grounds with father one Saturday afternoon, and as good fortune seemed to favor me I laid away in my pockets a good supply of cigar stumps for future use. That night I went to sleep on the floor as usual, and the next morning my trousers went into the dirty clothes and a clean pair was laid out ready when I got up. How I ever could have forgotten all day Sunday those precious bits tucked away in my other trousers' pockets I never knew, but this I remember: Monday morning when my trousers began to be swashed about in the tub a few stray cigar stumps soon rose to the surface. That aroused a spirit of research, and the pockets were finally turned inside out and emptied, like a turkey's gizzard, and then I had to explain as best I could why I had turned my trousers into a tobacco warehouse. Leaving the cigarette package to tell its own story, I went on, climbing fences and brushing an opening through clumps of alders and picking my way from bog to bog till I came to the old spring. Cautiously I crept up to it so as not to scare the little trout I took for granted would still be there, when splash went a good sized frog into the water. How many times that same frog, or one of his ancestors, had spoiled all my fun in that way, scared the trout and roiled the water all up! But never mind, the water cleared, and I was soon eating my luncheon of sardines and crackers beside the spring and living the past all over again. Close by was the rotten stump of that old golden sweet apple tree, which, in early summer, by its fruit had so many times made me know I had, as Carlyle says, that diabolical arrangement called a stomach.

But I could not sit there dreaming long, there were so many spots to visit; so picking some fennel from the same old bunch that was growing there thirty years ago, and how many more I don't know, I went on through "Johnson's Woods." There, between those two trees, we pinned up a shawl once for a stage curtain and played "Dolly Dutton." As I remember it, the only thing that marred the complete success of the performance was the failure of Dolly to stand in the palm of her father's right hand as he held it out at arm's length. In the troupe there were Dolly, her father and the stage manager, leaving an audience of two, and, as I was too small to act the part of Dolly's father, one of the big girls did that. She clasped her fingers together, and Dolly, a girl nearly as large, with one arm around her father's neck and one foot in her father's clasped hands, tried to balance herself there for an instant. Possibly the usual stage fright that accompanies a first appearance in public was the trouble, but more probably Dolly's unusual weight caused the collapse, for both father and daughter fell in a heap in the first act, and that part of the play had to be omitted. A short distance farther on, however, in the corner of the fence, a real tragedy once occurred. One noon at school, when the ground was covered with snow, we heard the report of a gun, and pretty soon some of the boys came running up and said a man had been shot, down in the lots. When we got there the body had been removed, but in the corner of the fence, where the man fell, were clots of his brain and large patches of bloody snow. Two men had been out hunting muskrats, and in climbing the fence the gun of one of the men was accidentally discharged, literally blowing out the brains of the other and leaving an indelible impression on mine. So on I wandered, picking Adam's cups, more full, as of old, with dead bugs than rain water, crossing lots by the same old paths, and jumping brooks at the same old spots, till I came back to the mill again. The front door was open and I walked in. The mill was practically empty. On the lower floor great holes remained

(155)

where the fulling mills had been removed, and in places the
rotten boards creaked and settled under my feet. Nowhere
was there anything but stagnation and decay. The water
from the flume came gushing through the rotten gates into the
mill, like the life blood from an open wound, and went splash-
ing down into the black wheel-pit, twenty-five feet below, but
the turbine wheel would not turn. The shafts were rusted in,
the belts were off, the wheels would not revolve and everything but the water was so dead. On the second, third, fourth
and fifth floors it was the same. The long rooms once filled
with clattering looms, spinning jacks and humming cards were
now empty, excepting here and there a dismantled loom or a
rusty card. There was the belt, now thrown off the card forever, that a playmate of mine once tried to throw off with his
leg and in so doing threw his life away. His trousers caught,
and he was thrown over the pulley, striking on his head. He
was carried home and never spoke afterwards, but the gurgling
sound that came to my ears as I waited outside his bed room
door haunted me for months and, in a way, endeared him to
me as nothing his sweet-tempered nature ever before had done.
The machinery, the vitals of a concern that once kept 200 hands
busy, sometimes day and night, was gone, and nothing but the
shell remained. I tried to get up into the belfry and with my
knuckles hit the old bell I had rung so many times, but the
door was nailed down. The old rope that used to occasionally
yank me off the floor still hung there, but I dare not pull it
for fear the rotten old belfry would come down over my head.
In the entries, the fire buckets, once filled with water, were
now swollen and empty, so many winters had they frozen
and thawed. Outside the mill the boards around the gaso-
meter I used to pound so often had rotted away, the earth had
tumbled in and braces only kept the iron posts from falling
over. Down through the village the tenements were empty,
the windows were boarded up or smashed in, chimneys were
leaning unsteadily and in some cases had fallen flat, and every-

where weeds were growing rank, bushes were springing up thick and the place was being choked to death. I went back to the house again, laid down under a pear tree and began to fill up and choke, too. Everything was either dying or already dead. The old home was going to decay; fruit trees I had helped to plant around it had grown up, borne fruit and died; Sleepy David, the horse I used to ride to school and made such a pet of, was gone, and Bruiser, the big New Foundland and St. Bernard dog I loved so, was dead, and yet I was left. Why was it? I was no better than they and in many ways not so good. How many mean things I did then and had done since. I had grown no better, nor was I, in some ways, so good now as I was then. Then I didn't know; now I do. Why had I been allowed to live? At the thought my heart seemed to burst with one great impulse, to ever after be good and do right. In no other way could the gratitude I felt be shown.

Gradually I began to think more and more of Bruiser and how I felt the day he was put under the pear tree near where I lay. How I wished that day he knew how sorry I was to have him go and how sorry I was too that I had ever whipped him. He was a good dog, an ever so much better dog than I was a boy. Yet I whipped him for not doing things I thought he ought to do. No one ever whipped me, though, for doing lots of things I ought never to have done. His faults were negative, mine positive. I whipped him for letting the muskrats get away when we were digging into their nests for them out in the pond, but I was as much to blame as he was for their getting away. Sometimes I whipped him for not digging for them when he knew (and I didn't) there were no muskrats there to dig for. To this day I am sorry for acting so and wish he knew it. But still he knew, or ought to, that I loved him the day he broke through the ice and came near drowning. He and I were over on the back side of the pond when my brother broke through on purpose down near the barn where it was shallow. Bruiser saw him and without a word from me started on the run across the pond, clawing into the thin ice and howling out in his agony to get to him.

He had scarcely reached the middle of the pond before he too, broke through. Then I was in a pickle. How I cried to my brother to hurry, and how I ran around on the bank in my anxiety! It took but a few minutes, but it seemed an age, for my brother to crawl out where he was, run around the pond, crawl out on his hands and knees and pull Bruiser, now completely exhausted, out by the nape of the neck. The great dog was too weak to shake himself much, but the rest of that day he was made a hero. This was not the first time Bruiser had started to rescue a boy from drowning. Once, when he was not two years old, without being told, he dragged a boy out of deep water, and yet, after living for sixteen years such a life, he is, as Byron says, of another noble Newfoundland, "denied in Heaven the soul he held on earth." Another time, when the ice was considerably thicker, I remember we made him draw a big party of us about the pond by his tail, and he enjoyed it as much as we did. We ran our sleigh out upon the ice and six or eight grown persons got in. Then I sat down on my sled between the thills, with one hand took hold of one thill, and, grabbing his tail with the other, beckoned off across the pond. The way he snaked that load of 1,200 or 1,500 pounds by his tail across the ice was not slow; and I recollect it was well we didn't go slow, for in crossing the channel the two sleigh runners left distinct marks where the ice had cracked under us, so thin was it. Then sometimes I would draw him on the sled, but he usually felt very humiliated by such proceeding. Several times we dressed him up with a coat and tied a beaver hat on and made him ride. Once he was sitting on the sled with the coat and hat on when a neighboring bulldog, for whom Bruiser harbored a deep-seated contempt, came along and began to growl derisively for such a ridiculous-looking object as Bruiser made upon the sled. I saw what was coming, and tried all I could to quiet Bruiser. He was just boiling over inside, and whining and licking his chops in his desire to get at his visitor. Finally, bursting all control, Bruiser sent the sled flying in one direction, pealed off his coat, burst the string that fastened on his hat, and, springing for the bulldog, he sent him home yelping in short order. Then he came back wagging his tail, wiping his lips and smiling, but occasionally glancing back sternly and growling. Lying under the tree, I began to recall how he used to lay down on the front doorstep, with his paws just hanging over the edge, and stay there for hours looking off toward the mill; how he used to persist in following the carriage every day but Sunday, when he religiously remained at home; and how, as he became more infirm and less strong in the legs, he insisted on riding, and would never be content with any but the front seat; and how he used to steal quietly upstairs Sunday morning and crawl into bed with us; and how—and—and—then I woke up, got out my machine and rode back to the city, in my soul feeling better for my pilgrimage to Windermere.

Christmas at Windermere.

CHRISTMAS was the day of all the year at Windermere, both a festive holiday and father's birthday. To us children, therefore, it had a double significance, and year by year we made more and more of it. Weeks before the event plans were laid and programmes arranged, but the sign which cast its shadow farthest before was the preparations made for trimming the rooms. To go out into the woods for the running and standing evergreens usually fell to my lot, and many a bushel, sometimes only to be found by digging down through the snow, did I pull up and back home in bags. This was wound into ropes and wreaths by us all during the winter evenings and the long coils of green were laid away on the cellar bottom and occasionally sprinkled to keep them fresh till Christmas came. The pop-corn, too, had to be strung, and when the time came it took a milk pan full of walnuts, one or two of butternuts and quite as much pop-corn to go around. Once an Irishman, one of the farm hands, offered to help me, but only once. That time he soon cracked his thumb open in place of the butternut, and the next instant the offending nut was crushed into pulp by a blow, this time savagely well directed. Another time, just for fun, I placed one of those wooden snakes in the bottom of the pan and covered it with pop-corn. Father was let into the secret, and after the folks had all gathered about the table and he had dished out some corn, he reached down and pulled out that wriggling, life-like reptile. One scream was uttered and the women folks sprang from the table in terror.

"How could you frighten us so," said one, giving me a look, and then I was sorry I did it.

Walnuts, butternuts and pop-corn came to be such a welcome dish during the winter evenings that scarcely a night passed, surely Sunday evening never, without one or the other, or, instead, apples and cider. These, except the cider which must be kept cool, I made ready directly after supper, and when we had all come together in the sitting room father generally read aloud to us, either the "Autocrat of the Breakfast table," one of Dickens', or perhaps some of J. G. Holland's works. All of Dickens', even twice over, he read to us in that way. Sometimes under the table, but usually the sofa, was my place. There I would lie and listen till, by 9 o'clock, I was generally sound asleep. But regularly as I went to sleep it was never necessary for father, like good old Wardle, to say,

" Joe, Joe, damn that boy, he's asleep again," when it came time for the cider and popcorn. Like the close of a sermon, the sudden stillness that came over the room as father ceased reading, followed soon after by the thin, small voice of the cider down in the cellar directly underneath, a voice that grew in tone deeper and deeper as the pitcher gradually filled up, this, without further warning, always served to arouse me to the occasion and to the pop-corn and cider. Along towards spring, when the cider had grown hard, a barrel of ale usually found its way into the cellar, and those evenings with Dickens', followed by pop-corn, walnuts or apples and the whole topped off with a glass of nose tingling cider or foaming ale, came to be a part of our very life at Windermere.

But as to Christmas and the preparations for it. First there was the comb orchestra. Father, with a coarse bass comb covered with tissue paper, hummed the tune through it, while Florine accompanied him on the piano, Minnie with the accordion, Dassa with the tambourine and myself with the triangle. Occasionally the entire orchestra used combs of different sizes and the reedy effect then was really fine. Let me live over again one of those Christmas Eves, seen as it was then through my boyish eyes and recalled now more than a quarter of a century later.

All day long we had been busy getting things ready;

(161)

father in the parlors suggesting this and helping about that; mother in the kitchen preparing for the event which never failed to come up to our expectations, the turkey or game supper; Adelbert dragging in the trees and fastening them up; Florine, Minnie, Dassa, Jeffie and Jennie arranging the evergreens, and myself heaping pan after pan of walnuts, butternuts and pop-corn (salted while it was hot) and wiping off the apples till they shone like wax. And then, when everything inside was finished and the parlors had been swept out and set to rights, how anxious I began to feel for fear the company would not all come. The candles in the windows, one in each of the small panes on the front of the house, had been lighted, the blinds had been thrown wide open and I stood in the hall near the front door waiting for the sound of the bells. Outside the paths had been dug wide and deep even to the middle of the road, the lantern had been placed upon the gate post and the flaring candles in the windows lit up the snow round about as bright as day

The bells stopped, and I rushed out, followed to the door by Florine, Minnie and the rest.

"Chush!" cried a girl's voice out in the sleigh. "Chush, chush," came the ready answer to the countersign from the front door, and then we knew Alice was there and that the Farmers had come. They always came first. My work was to pilot the men folks around to the barn with the lantern, and see that their horses were comfortably tucked up with blankets under the shed. It would never do to let one of those horses, now throwing off clouds of steam in the frosty air, catch cold, and so all our sleighs and wagons had been run out of the shed into the snow to make room for them.

More bells coming; but those didn't stop. The next ones did. "Hello, there!" cried father at the door.

"Can you keep a couple here over night?" asked a voice out in the snow, accompanied with a well-known laugh, and then we knew the McKinneys had come.

Again some bells stopped, and the Seldens were here. But the ones I looked for more than all else were late, but, if late, the Henrys finally came, and then I was happy.

Once here and all in the sitting room together, they were not long in getting warm, and then the Christmas entertainment began. The double doors into the front parlor were thrown open, and a pretty sight it was. The room had been festooned around the side and into the center overhead with cables of evergreen; the windows, glaring with candles, had been hung with wreaths and crosses, and the two trees at the further end of the room, tastefully trimmed with the stringed pop-corn and sparkling with burning tapers and tiny reflectors, made a brilliant background, in front of which was the comb orchestra.

"Fisher's Hornpipe," "Money Musk," and one or two other selections were given without more ado but with a snap that set everyone on tiptoe. Even Henry Johnson, an asthmatic colored man, going by the house one Christmas Eve, was so stirred with the music that he stopped and danced for full five minutes in the deep snow all alone. The program, printed and distributed among the audience, was then carried out. First was Santa Claus' address. Adelbert, when the doors were again opened, appeared as an old colored dwarf, wearing glasses and standing upon a table. He really stood behind it with his hands in a pair of boots that rested upon the table. His vest was drawn on over his arms so as to conceal them, and directly behind him hung a dark curtain. Behind the curtain stood Dassa with her arms thrust through it and coming out over his shoulders, her arms answering for his. Occasionally during the address, a boot was raised to emphasize some point, and an umbrella in Dassa's hand was brought down across the table with a whack.

"Bretherin and Sisterin," he said, "I propose to discourse to you on dis suspicious occasion from de two eyed chapter ob de one eyed John in which you will find de followin' words: 'We come to wallop (stamps with his foot)

(163)

Cæsar, not to praise him.' To stand under dis soapjack perfectly we will divide de 'scourse into severial heads. Fustly and fomostly de Cæsar who is represented on dis occasion is not de Cæsar who fit, bled and died in history, but a white pusson who has seen but forty-six summers and no winters to speak of. (If dem dare chillens ober dare in de corner don't stop dey will break de subject of de'scourse). Having sufficiently elucidated to your benighted minds who Cæsar am we will now proceed to 'cuss de main point of dis summon. Cæsar shall be walloped (stamps). 'Cause why? (groans). Fustly, 'cause he was such a idiotic fool as to show hisself in dis world 46 years ago dis blessed minute, six hours hence. And secondly if we don't wallop Cæsar he will wallop us. (If dem chillen in de corner don't hush, tote 'em out.) Finally and lastly how and when shall Cæsar be walloped? My feller hearers, I tell you he is a tough cuss (stamps). I repeat, he is a tough customer. My bruder dough-heads, de shingle must be used and dat freely. Spare de shingle and spile de chile, or, as Solomon says in another of de same chapter, ' Lay on, Mickey Duffy and damned be he who fust cries, Holt, enuff.' My hearers, you must seize time by de windpipe and when de clock strikes de witching hour of 12, let him feel de application of dis summon in person."

The address was received with hearty applause and was delivered without serious interruption. Once, Dassa had some difficulty in readjusting the spectacles on Adelbert's nose, and once she turned over two leaves of the manuscript at one time, but as she was behind the curtain and could not see what she had done, the only way Adelbert could communicate the fact was by gently kicking her in the shins.

Two or three tableaux followed: one, " Past and Future," by Florine and Alice; another, "Yankee Courtship," by Walton, Minnie and Jennie, and " The Course of True Love," by Minnie, Alice, Walton and Adelbert. Next on the programme was a song by Mr. Henry, "The Brave Old Hoak;" the

"Black Crook Dance," by Mr. Selden, and the "Jolly Jig," by Mr. McKinney. Two or three shadow pantomimes were shown upon the sheet hung up in the double doors, and "Hard Times," "Bold Morgan McCarty" and "Hush a Bye Baby" completed the musical part of the programme. Adelbert and I, with a blanket thrown over us and small eyes pinned on outside and an imitation trunk in front, made a very fair looking elephant as we passed through the rooms; and I came in alone as a "night howler," rigged up to represent some Paleozoic reptile and making an ˌunearthly noise by means of a whistle in my mouth. The presents (one year amounting in value to $1,700) were distributed from the trees and then we went out to supper.

Roast turkey, chicken pie, succotash (a rare dish for the season), brown bread, boiled onions, squash, mashed potatoes and turnips, celery and cake, coffee and mince pie, walnuts, butternuts, apples and cider—that was the supper. The old folks had one table, and we young folks another all by ourselves and didn't we have a good time. It wasn't long before we got to laughing and then every little thing would set us off. The old folks were slow to offer toasts, and mother, to whom was due the excellence of the supper, was about the only one besides father that was remembered at that table. But with us, long before the cider came round, we were drinking coffee and even cold water to everybody.

The "Bloody Sixty-ninth" came to be the favorite. "Here's to the Bloody Sixty-ninth. The last in the fayld and the first to lave it," cried some one and then we all stood up. Hardly had we become seated before some one else gave the same toast as amended by a brother Irishman:

"Here's to the Bloody Sixty-ninth. Aqual to none." Then one of us said: "Here's to Mr. McKinney" and some one, Chauncey, I think, promptly added, "Aqual to none." Then how Mr. McKinney laughed, ending as he always did by laughing himself into a cough.

CHRISTMAS AT WINDERMERE.

" Here's to Mr. Henry," ventured some one else, and with one accord a dozen young voices added, "Aqual to none " That made us laugh till we nearly cried. So it went. Mr. Farmer was found "Aqual to none " and so was Mr. Selden. Father came in for fully his share. When, however, some one happened to think of Bruiser and said, " Here's to old Bruiser," the table rattled and the glasses jingled as they never did before and the unction with which we added the inevitable "Aqual to none " showed how strong a hold he, too, had upon our affections.

But the pointers drew around to 12 only too soon and the last number on the programme was yet to be carried out A few minutes after midnight, when most of the party had returned to the sitting room, father was suddenly grabbed by three or four and down he went. Out came the slippers and blow upon blow rained down upon him. In the midst of the struggle I saw Adelbert holding him fast while the others laid on the counts, " Thirty-one, thirty-two," and unable to remain quiet any longer, in a twinkling I had Adelbert by the legs and down he went too. Turning promptly he soon had me standing on my head, but even then I had the satisfaction of knowing I had diverted his attention from father for a time. But they all were too much for him and soon the count had run up to " Forty-four, forty-five, forty-six " and the blows ceased. The " Downfall of the Head of the House," the last number on the programme had been successfully carried out and soon after the different sleighs, one after another, were brought around, the occupants were snugly tucked in, the horses started off impatiently, the bells jingled away in the distance and one more Christmas eve was gone.

INDEX.

(167)

INDEX.

(171

INDEX.

(172)

LITTLEFIELD, Jane, 71.
    "   Rebecca, 71, 72, 80.
LORING, Mary, 51.
LOTHRUP, Rev. John, 102.
LUDDEN, Alice, 51, 73.
  " Benjamin, 51, 73, 74, 111.
  "   " 2nd, 51, 74, 111, 115.
  " Eunice, 10, 25, 74, 81, 85, 96, 111, 115.
  "   " H., 74.
  " James, 51, 73.
  " Sarah, 51, 74, 111, 115.

MANN, Frances H., 67, 75.
  " Mary, 21, 52, 67, 75.
  " William, 21, 52, 67, 75.
MARBURY, Agnes I., 36, 76.
  " Bridget D., 76, 102.
  " Catherine, 37, 76, 79, 102.
  " Rev. Francis, 36, 37, 76, 77, 102.
  " William, 36, 76.
MASHAM, Sir William, 143, 145.
MEIRIC 18.
  " ap Arthur, 18.
MOSELEY, Elizabeth, 87.
MOORE, " 76.
MOTT, Ann S., 72, 80.
  " Elizabeth, 72, 80.
  " Nathaniel, 72, 80.
MOWRY, Hannah, 63, 84, 108.
  " Joanna I., 20, 81.
  " John, 54, 83, 92.
  " Mary J., 54, 81, 83, 84, 90, 108.
  " " 2nd, 10, 20, 55, 81, 82, 83, 92.
  " " 3rd, 83, 92.
  " Nathaniel, 20, 54, 55, 81.
  " Roger, 54, 63, 81, 83, 84, 108.
MULLINS, Joseph, 85.
  " Priscilla, 9, 85.
  " William, 9, 85.

NESTA, 18.
NILES, widow, 115.

(174)

INDEX.

---

* See page 42. This sketch is the only one about which the writer retains any reasonable or serious doubt, but, after considerable research, he is satisfied the conclusion arrived at is approximately correct.